BELLY UP

BELLY UP

STORIES

RITA BULLWINKEL

A STRⱯNGE
ȮBJECT
Austin, Texas

The stories in this collection have appeared in slightly different forms in the following publications:

"Phylum" in *BOMB*, "Black Tongue" in *Conjunctions*, "Nave" in *Deep South Magazine*, "Hunker Down" in the *Fanzine*, "Decor" in *Tin House*, "Concerned Humans" in *Native Magazine*, "In the South, the Sand Winds Are Our Greatest Enemy" in *Joyland*, "Passing" in the *Conium Review*, "Mouth Full of Fish" in *Spork*, and "What Girl Built" in *The Brooklyn Rail*.

Published by
A Strange Object
astrangeobject.com
© 2018 Rita Bullwinkel. All rights reserved.
First paperback edition April 2018
Printed in the United States of America.

9 8 7 6 5 4 3 2

ISBN 978-0-9985184-3-5
IBSN 978-0-9985184-4-2 (ebook)

This is a work of fiction. Any resemblances to actual persons, living or dead, events, or locales are coincidental.

Cover art by Geoff McFetridge
Cover design by Kelly Winton
Book design by Amber Morena

After Ann Bullwinkel

CONTENTS

BELLY UP

HARP
\\\\\\\\\\\\\\\\\\\

A BOY I DATED IN COLLEGE had an uncle who worked for an oil company in Malaysia. The uncle was frequently gone to Malaysia on business. He died suddenly, and they found out he had a wife and family there. He also had a wife and family here. The boyfriend said the uncle had split himself clean in two. Perhaps he changed clothes on the plane ride over. It was hard to tell. Nobody ever went with the uncle to Malaysia and nobody ever met the Malaysian wife.

I remembered the story one morning during my commute. I have a long drive on a pretty highway to get me to the building where I work. When I first moved out of the city I hated the drive. But it grew on me. It became a time for me to be alone and listen to music my husband maybe wouldn't have liked, or even to listen to music I wouldn't have wanted my husband to know I listened to.

I remembered the story when I saw an accident. It happened just two cars in front of me, fast enough that I wasn't caught in the back-up behind the accident, but had to swerve away from other swerving cars. When I looked in my rearview mirror I saw the pile up, and the front windshield of one car smashed in and two heads, one on the steering wheel of the wrecked car, unmoving, and one of a woman in the passenger seat. She was wearing a headscarf and her mouth was open. It looked like she was screaming. She didn't look to the man next to her, the one whose head was on the wheel, but rather everywhere else. This is the Malaysian wife, I thought. That's why she isn't looking at the husband. Because her troubles have begun.

Though when I saw the accident I remembered that the Malaysian wife existed, I couldn't immediately remember to whom she belonged. A decade had passed since the story had first been told to me, and I couldn't place her with a person of origin until later in the day. The remembering of her wasn't unpleasant as much as curious. I tried to remember what I thought of the story when it had originally been told to me. I didn't call my husband and tell him about the accident or the remembering. It was too strange of a thing to remember not to be upsetting. Not that I was upset. But I just didn't want to be forced into making words on the subject, especially since I couldn't parse out whom I cared about more—the halved uncle or the Malaysian wife.

The day I saw the accident I got to work on time. I am a secretary in the music department of a big university. When I arrived, I went into the staff kitchen and put my lunch in the refrigerator, and then walked down the hall to get some water. On my walk to the water fountain I heard several harps tuning.

I know little about music, but I like working in a building whose sole purpose is to produce it. The classrooms closest to my office are mainly musical instruction spaces. I hear trumpets and timpani throughout the day.

The harps, though, were something new. Days previous I had seen them roll in a dozen of them. They were huge. A single person couldn't lift one. They had to be transported with a wheeled cart. All of the harps' scrolls had grand, circular, crownlike adornments atop them. Their peaks looked like small royal heads.

I have heard a harp before, but this tuning sound they were making as I walked past was completely alien. It made me feel like a different person—like I, the person listening to the tuning of these harps, was a different person than the person who had been standing next to the refrigerator in the lunchroom. I have had this feeling while listening to music before. Always, it was at some crowded concert. At these shows the music had always been loud and inciting, music that made me feel like I was the kind of person who could hit someone. But the person the harps made me into wouldn't have hit anyone. I wasn't sure the harp me would have any hands to hit with. It was as if my soul had been slipped into a new harp body, some shell that existed primarily in vibrations and could more easily mix with the objects and people it chose to surround. Listening to the harps, I didn't feel angry or sad or anxious or incited. I just felt other than myself.

Gradually, the voice of the harp professor rose and all of the harps stopped tuning. Hush returned and I continued the walk back down the hall. I sat down at my desk and thought about my harp self and the Malaysian wife.

Although I still couldn't remember who told me the story, I remembered what I had thought when I had first heard it. I had thought about the Malaysian children: the children of the Malaysian wife and her halved American husband. I had felt sorry for the children that they would have to live a life without a father. I felt sorry for the Malaysian wife, that her husband—and, in my imagination, her main source of income—had died, and that now she was being left to fend for herself and her children alone in some Malaysian city. I did not conceive of the Malaysian wife as having parents or siblings. I assumed she was completely alone. I imagined she had been preyed upon. She had been a young, gullible woman—the kind of woman who always thinks everything is going to turn out all right. The kind of woman who would marry a man who spoke her native language poorly. Perhaps this tendency in her also made her susceptible to religion. Maybe she was devout. Maybe she wore a headscarf. Maybe she liked American television. Maybe the husband had looked like a famous American actor. Or, maybe he didn't look like an actor at all, but he was American and that was enough.

I sat down at my desk and sank into the seat. I called hotels and made reservations for music professors who were performing abroad. I checked the faculty mailboxes and emailed the professors whose boxes were bursting. I emailed the department about an upcoming concerto. I emailed the department about a visiting lecturer. I emailed the department about senior recitals. I had lunch.

I ate my lunch outside on a park bench. I stretched my legs out and let them warm in the early spring heat. It was March, still the time of year when it was appropriate to wear tights, but I wasn't wearing any. After I ate my sandwich I looked at the sun through the trees and, in a moment of daring, decided to lie down. I tilted my head back and swung my legs up and put my hands over my face to shield my eyes from the sun. A breeze wove through the leaves, and the hairs on my arms stood up. The longer I reclined, however, the warmer I felt. The sun beat on my face and my legs. I wished I could stay there, lying on that park bench, pretending that I was the kind of person who always lay down in public spaces, as if it hadn't been an act of daring brought on by a morning filled with the remembering of the Malaysian wife.

I eventually got up and walked back to my building. I rode the elevator alone. I had been hoping that someone would be with me in the elevator—that I would run into someone I knew and they would say, "Hello, Helen, how are you today?" and then I would be able to tell them about the accident. I wasn't upset about the accident, but I had seen a person die, I was almost sure. The man's head against the wheel had looked very dead. And I really don't know how you are supposed to act when something like that happens. It is very unclear what is socially acceptable and what is not. Because I am a secretary for the music department, I rarely speak to people unless a professor seeks me out to make a particularly large round of copies. And even then, my interactions are quick. People have things to do. And I guess I do too.

When I got out of the elevator I walked down the hall that contained the new harp practice room. I looked through the small glass window of the practice room door and saw that the room was empty. I went in and sat down at one of the harps.

Up close they looked less like instruments and more like massive pieces of furniture—like some grand decorative hat stand or an unfinished shelf. Strangely, they also looked like instruments you could dance with, like how upright bass players sometimes swing their instruments around in emotive grooves. I wondered why harp players are always seated. Maybe the seated harp playing position was just some outdated invention of Western civilization, like the expectation for women to give birth on their backs. Maybe a harp was meant to be played standing up. Maybe a harp was meant to be danced with. Maybe these people had it all wrong. I ran my finger along the spine of each one of the harp's strings and fingered the carvings in the neck.

I went back to my desk and sat down. I put together packets for letters of admittance. I ordered several music journals for the department library. I stapled syllabi for several classes. I alphabetized the hundreds of scores contained in Professor Robinson's filing cabinet. I cleaned the outside of the cabinet with a damp cloth. I called my husband.

"Hello," my husband said. "How was your morning?"

"My morning was fine," I said. "What are we eating for dinner?"

"Pork chops," said my husband.

On the drive home there was no traffic. The budding trees overhung the highway and the black granite boulders reflected white light from the sun.

I passed the spot where the accident had happened. All of the debris was gone. I wondered where they took the body that belonged to the man whose head was on the wheel. I wondered where they took his wife. I imagined the morgue that the husband lay contained in, all the rows of file cabinet refrigerators. I imagined the file cabinets that were filled with scores in the music department instead being filled with dead halved bodies, the cabinets in Professor Robinson's office pulling out into much longer trays than their dimensions contained. I imagined opening the cabinets and cleaning the space between the two halves of the bodies with a warm damp cloth. I saw myself closing the cabinets and going back to the harp room. All the students were in the room with me, tuning. I sat in the tuning harp sounds and became the harp me.

I arrived home in my car and went inside and took off my jacket and drank a glass of water. I took out my laptop and searched for upcoming harp performances and saw that the city orchestra was having a Celtic harp orchestra performance tomorrow night. I bought two tickets.

I wanted to take a shower before my husband returned home so I went into the bathroom and took off my clothes. The hot water pulled over my head and my eyes and I stood perfectly still. I like the feeling of being encased in water, and I like feeling the pressure of pumped water against my closed eyes. I tilted my neck back and let some of the water enter my mouth. I swallowed the hot water and thought about it traveling down inside of me while the other hot water traversed the curve of my spine.

In the shower I remembered who the Malaysian wife belonged to. The college boyfriend's original telling of the story was all of a sudden clear. I remembered the color of the couch the boyfriend sat on when he first told the story. It had been a deep forest green. We were with a large group of friends. He nervously leaned toward me and made a joke about his family. Then he told the story of the halved uncle and everything got very quiet and it almost sounded as if he was going to cry. I said the night was too deep in for these conversations and smiled encouragingly and asked him to walk me home. That night he slept in my apartment. I didn't have a bedframe so my mattress was on the floor. When we went to sleep he was unusually quiet but I couldn't tell if it was because he was drunk or because his telling of the story had upset him. I didn't know his parents, so I didn't know who he thought this story reflected on poorly. I wasn't sure if he felt some type of internal guilt or responsibility for sharing blood with this uncle, or if he felt he had divulged something like a family history of insanity, and now thought I could never look at him the same. He lay in my bed with his back toward me.

His breathing was steady so I couldn't tell if he was awake or asleep. I pulled my fingers over his scalp and behind his ears and into the dent of his spine. I put both my hands into his hair and pressed my lips against the back of his neck. We fell asleep like that. I remembered waking up in the morning cradling his head.

The water turned cold in the shower. I turned off the water and heard my husband chopping vegetables in the next room.

I got out of the shower, dried my hair and dressed for dinner. I came out of our bedroom and kissed my husband on the cheek. He was making a grand meal. The salad had goat cheese and candied pecans and cranberries in it. The pork chops were seared and dressed in gravy. Mashed potatoes with scallions were on the side. I sat down and looked at my husband. I said, "This meal looks divine."

"Thank you," my husband said. "How was your day?"

"Well," I said. "It was good, but something upsetting happened to a coworker. Her brother died."

"Oh my goodness," my husband said. "That's terrible. Was he young?"

"Yes, quite young. He was 37. He was an oil-rig engineer. He spent a lot of time working in Malaysia."

"What did he die of?" my husband asked.

"He died of a heart attack."

"Did he die in Malaysia or here?"

"He died in Malaysia. No one in her family knows yet who is going to get the body."

"Well we should offer to make her and her family dinner," my husband said.

"You're right."

After dinner I cleaned the dishes while my husband read. I put on some music and tried to read as well but felt restless and eventually put on my tennis shoes and decided to go for a walk.

"I'm going for a walk," I said to my husband.

"Are you all right? Would you like me to come with you?"

"I think I just need to take a quick walk alone."

I put on my sweatshirt and closed the door softly behind me. I walked down our street and kicked some branches that had fallen into the road.

I thought of the boyfriend with the halved uncle and tried to remember what I thought of the boyfriend. We had not dated for long. I remembered him being very insecure and always trying to overestablish himself in conversations. He seemed to have a lot of feelings, but a poor system of making them known. He was only a boy when I had known him. Perhaps this tendency of his had changed.

As I walked in my neighborhood it occurred to me that maybe he had lied to me. Maybe there was no Malaysian wife. Maybe it was a story he made up to win attention. He seemed like the type of boy who would do such a thing— the type of boy who, when he knew that a girl was no longer interested in sleeping with him, would make up a story about being beaten by his father just to gain her pity. The type of boy who didn't mind appearing broken to lovers, and even hoped that his brokenness would entice new lovers to want to fix him.

I thought of his face when he had told the story and

tried to discern if there had been any truth in him. I decided I couldn't tell, or, at the very least, I couldn't really remember his face. And then I decided the truth didn't matter. Surely there had been a Malaysian wife somewhere, some version of her at least existed in my mind and, very possibly, in the wreckage of the car which I had seen crash in the morning.

I walked back to my house and did some laundry. I took off my clothes and read some of a book in bed. My husband came in and laid his body next to me. He went to sleep.

I sat in the bed next to my husband. I tried to sleep and then got up and got something to drink. I sat in our dark kitchen. The sky was clear and light. I drew a picture of my husband and me on a paper napkin. I tried to parse out who I cared about more, the halved husband or the Malaysian wife.

The thing about caring about someone is that it doesn't necessarily follow that you agree with them, or think they are morally right. Caring is an act of interest. The Malaysian wife certainly did not have a good life. She married a man who gave her children that he didn't care for. He left them and died. I supposed my interest in caring for the Malaysian wife hinged on her community. How she lived with the halved husband, how life was with him and then without him. Her predicament was terrible, but I decided it didn't interest me. What interested me was the halved husband, and the methods and techniques he used for halving himself. Or, the heinous, looming idea that he contained—the idea that some humans might need to be halved. That true love toward a single lover is an inherent lie. So, I decided I cared for the halved husband more, but that I hated him.

I thought then, for the first time that day, of the American wife. I thought of the apartment that she and her halved husband lived in, and of the TV they owned, and the water bill they paid, and the way they shared towels. I wondered if she could continue to love him in death. I wondered if she could love the half of the husband that had lived with her. I wondered how and when she got the body. I wondered if and how she held the ceremony. If I were the American wife I would cut the body in two lengthwise and send one half back to the Malaysian wife. Fair is fair.

In the early light of the morning I decided I didn't hate the halved husband for widowing two wives and orphaning some Malaysian children as much as I hated him for being halved. This is the kind of hate people have when their morality is challenged, I thought. I hate the halved husband because he hates the way I live.

I went back into the bedroom where my husband was still asleep. I put on my work clothes and kissed him on the cheek. I whispered in his ear, "Professor Robinson called. There is an emergency. I have to go into work early."

"All right," my husband said. "Well, make them let you off at a decent hour. Tonight I want to make you duck and beans."

I took some toast and walked out the door and into my car. When I got in the car I called my work. I got the answering machine, as I knew I would. I left a message. I said, "Hi Professor Robinson, this is Helen. I am sorry to tell you this on such short notice, but I won't be able to come in to work today. My husband's brother died unexpectedly last night, and I really have to stay here, at home with him. I should be able to come in tomorrow, but I will let you know."

After I hung up the phone I drove into the city. I drove on the highway where the accident had been and sped past the absence of debris. Once in the city, I parked the car in the underground of a mall. I got out of the car and went into the mall and into several stores. I tried on underwear and dresses and shoes and coats. I bought everything I wanted. I walked out wearing new earrings, a new dress and new shoes. I walked to the park and lay down on the park bench. The sun was warmer than it had been the day before. I got up and went to lunch in a nice restaurant. I ordered French onion soup and braised lamb for a main. There was a handsome man about my age sitting next to me. He said, "How is the lamb?"

"Delicious," I said. "Would you like a bite?"

"You know, I would. Mind if I join your table?"

"Please."

A waiter came over and we asked to have the man's plate moved to my table. I took the man's fork and cut him a piece of meat.

"This meat is amazing," he said.

"Wait till you taste the soup." I took a piece of bread from the breadbasket and dipped it in the bowl, making sure that the broth soaked up into it and that it was properly coated with cheese.

I handed it to the man, and he took it from me and said, "You're right. The soup is better than the lamb. I could eat a whole lunch of French onion soup. Next time."

We made plans to meet back at the same restaurant for dinner. I told him I had tickets to a harp show and invited him to go. We planned to eat dinner early so we could be on time for the harp tuning. I told him all about how I worked in the music building, and how listening to the sound of harps tuning made me feel so other, like another me, and that it was beautiful, I thought, and that I thought he would like it and we should go.

The man agreed to the harp concert and looked genuinely eager. He left and went back to his office and I got up and walked out into the street. Three blocks away there was a movie theater. I went in and watched a movie that was essentially *Hamlet* but set in Detroit. Inside the movie theater the seats were sticky. The fabric pulled up when I lifted my hand. The screen made everyone's faces look blue and pretty. Inside the movie theater I felt like I had nicer skin. If only I could be the harp me with a movie exterior, I thought. Maybe I could be.

While watching the movie I remembered the halved husband that I cared for and his wives. I wondered which wife he liked better. It would appear that because he married the Malaysian wife after the American wife he liked the Malaysian wife better. But maybe it was a relationship of geographic convenience. I found myself wishing that my husband was in the movie theater with me. I wanted him to put his hand on my thigh in the dark.

When the movie was over, I walked out of the movie

theater and into the dusk of the city. I stood under a lamp-post and watched the people pass by. I took my phone out of my pocket and called my husband. He said, "Helen? Are you coming home?"

"No," I said. "It's a big disaster. I hope I don't have to stay all night. Keep some duck warm in the oven for me. I'll be home as soon as I can."

After I hung up the phone, I walked back to the restaurant. I was a half hour early for dinner so I had a drink at the bar. I wondered why I hadn't ever asked the college boyfriend about the children. Had I believed that the children were beside the point? Did I always believe children were beside the point?

Sitting there at the bar, drinking my wine, I justified caring about the halved husband more than I cared about the children because the halved husband was a novelty, a rare two-headed snake to be brought up only late into the night at the most intimate of dinner parties when the conversation has gotten too serious and everyone is almost ready to go home. Orphaned children, on the other hand, are common emotional currency.

I wondered what my husband would think of the halved husband, though I, of course, had no intention of ever asking him. Many times what you think someone would say on a subject is much truer than the words that would actually come out of their mouth. My husband would probably be overly occupied with making sure all the parties were taken care of. If he could figure out a way to make the Malaysian wife and the American wife friends he probably would. What a rancid want. Who would want to meet the partial owner of a husband they believed to belong solely to them? My husband is the only optimist I know who would be blind enough to suggest such a meeting. I was glad I hadn't invited my husband to the harp concert. He probably would have just made tiresome comments speculating on the manufacturing techniques employed to fabricate the theater seats.

I put my wine glass down. The man from lunch walked into the restaurant and we sat at a nice table near a window. He told me his name was Huck, which I told him I found hard to believe.

"Like Huck Finn," I said.

"Exactly," said Huck.

Huck told me all about his day as a website designer. I told Huck all about my day as a secretary for a music department. I told him about the applications I had filed, and the staff meeting notes I had typed, and the plane flights I had changed for Professor Robinson's quartet.

Huck told me about his day writing code and tried to make it sound more important than it was, which I found silly. Huck became more enjoyable when he started talking about his family. His mother was an old Polish woman who lived in Queens. You could tell he loved her by the way he made fun of her. I asked him if I could come over for pierogi sometime and he said, of course.

We took a cab to the concert hall because the dinner had gotten away from us. We rushed to our seats as the first harps were being carted in. Slowly the musicians unwrapped them from their big jackets and started tuning. There were eighteen harps in total, which was absolutely grand. When the harps started tuning, I felt the other me ecstasy returning. I wished I could walk around with these sounds for the rest of my life. While the harps tuned nothing was required of me. I thought of all the things my husband needs from me. I have to speak to my husband and cook with him. I have to use words to tell him what I feel. Sometimes my husband needs me to reassure him. The easiest thing I have ever done with my husband was lovemaking. That has never been tiresome or hard to do. I wondered if maybe I should suggest that my husband and I stop talking. Perhaps we should only communicate through touch and feel. Maybe that is a truer way to be with someone. Maybe my husband and I just needed to rid ourselves of words and then we could access something more intimate. I found myself truly resenting the pockets of meaning each word I hurled at my husband was meant to communicate. Why couldn't I just take my raw feeling and give it to him? Why was I required to translate something within me into a symbol that an uncountable number of humans have used before me and will use again?

While the harps were tuning Huck wanted to keep talking.

"Shhhh," I said to Huck. "I am listening to the tuning."

He looked confused but not altogether saddened. He closed his eyes and tried to turn into harp Huck, but I could tell he wasn't having a good time.

Eventually the harps stopped tuning and started playing in earnest. I liked the choreographed coordination of their strings as well, although it didn't induce the same other me.

After the show I kissed Huck goodbye and told him next time we'd see a rock show. Then I started my long walk back to the parking lot under the mall. I crossed lonely streets strewn with trash and flyers. Every couple blocks I passed a waking bar.

While I walked I saw two young boys playing cards in an alley. They were about fifteen, and surely lived in one of the buildings nearby. The younger looking one whistled at me. He looked like a young Huck and my husband combined.

When I got to my car, I was tired. I had walked and been awake for so long. I got into my car and drove along the deserted streets. I weaved in and out of the city blocks aimlessly and then, when my lids began to droop, I found the nearest highway entrance and began my regular commute home.

I love driving on the freeway when everyone else is absent. I thought maybe I should start commuting at night. I sped along the freeway and passed the trees and the rocks that looked so stunning in the daylight. At night they weren't as beautiful. Instead of feeling like a canopy from the sun they felt like a dark cloak. Their black arms reached over the road and threatened to engulf me. I put my chin over the wheel and leaned forward so I could see the foliage on both sides in one view. I fingered the stereo in longing and made a mental note that I had to find a recording of the harps tuning. Perhaps I could befriend the harp professor and convince her to make a recording for a charitable cause. Or, I could see her being the kind of woman who was suspicious of charity. Maybe we could become friends in earnest and I could tell her about the harp me.

As I neared the spot where the accident had happened I slowed down. Someone had put a cross and a bouquet of lilies on the side of the road. I stopped the car in the middle of the freeway and beamed my lights on the memorial. A long shadow pulled out from the cross and I saw that there were more offerings scattered about.

After sitting in the car for several moments in stark silence I decided to pull off and investigate. I drove the car off the road and under the overhang of a tree. I walked the fifty feet back to the memorial site. When I got there I saw that there were indeed many more flowers. Amaryllis and baby's breath were scattered all around. It looked like they had all been a part of the same bouquet and then the wind had gotten a hold of them. In the dark the baby's breath looked like clumps of cloud.

I looked at this memorial for the man whose head was on the wheel, the man who crashed and made me remember the halved husband. The man who crashed and made me remember the Malaysian wife. I tried to understand in what ways this memorial was and was not for the halved husband of my imagination. Could every husband be partially halved in some way? I decided I needed to seek counsel with the halved husband and sat down next to his memorial. First I sat with my legs pulled up to my chest and addressed his cross directly, but then I grew tired and lay down. I spread out all my limbs on the ground like I was making a snow angel. I tried to pull myself apart from the inside out. I imagined all my organs choosing a side and then willing my sternum open. I made harp tuning sounds with my mouth and sung into the split. I could feel the halved husband helping me form two new bodies. His hands gripped the inside of my ribs and pulled up. I kept humming until I could feel that the separation was finished. When I was finally halved and happy, I put my two selves back in the car and started the engine. I turned on the radio and listened to a heavy beat. A great relief washed over me. I knew then I could do what I wanted. I knew then that the reason I hated the halved husband so much was not because he hated the way I lived, but because I envied him. Now that I too was halved, I had no resentment toward him.

I got up and drove home and got into bed with my husband. I woke him early in the morning and we made love. He cooked me a hearty breakfast of eggs and bacon. Before I went to work, I held him in the doorway. I put my hands into his hair and felt the back of his skull. I pulled his body towards mine and put my own head into the crook of his shoulder.

While driving back into the city, I listened to music. I turned the radio to a classical station that mostly played Brahms. When I was two blocks away from my work building I was stopped by a red light at a big intersection. A couple stepped off the sidewalk and traversed the street. The woman was wearing a headscarf and the man was wearing a suit. They took their time crossing. When the light turned green they were directly in front of my bumper. They were walking so slow. I wished they would hurry up. Didn't they know this was a city? People have to get places. I didn't have all day to wait for them. When it became clear that they truly would take all day if the day was given to them, I honked my horn and made my eyes bulge out and look at them. Surprised by the sudden noise they jumped, stared into the windshield, and then hurried on.

PHYLUM
\\\\\\\\\\\\\\\\\\

I WAS THE TYPE OF MAN who got his ears cleaned. I was the type of woman who didn't like dogs. We lived together in a house on a street that was the color of asphalt. I told you what I thought of you. I told you to leave me alone. You didn't own the house. I never liked our street. It smelled like cough syrup. I like living in a place that smells good.

I was the type of man who went to board meetings. I was the type of woman who liked gouda cheese. We lived together in an apartment next to a deli. I stole money from your wallet. I knew you hated how I dressed. I snuck out in the night and went to Harlem. The thing about cities is anyone can go anywhere and never be seen. We both knew it made the game easier. We both liked knowing there was a game.

I was the type of woman who liked swimming in hotel pools. I was the type of man who liked listening to plays. We didn't have children. You listened to Mozart and Bach, and always said you loved classical music, but I knew, and you knew that you don't know any other composers. I like John Lennon. That isn't a composer. Says who?

I was the type of man who walked out into the night and took my hair in my hands and dropped to my knees and wept. I was the type of woman who recycled every scrap of waste I ever produced because the thought that I was slowly killing our planet made me feel like my intestines were climbing up my throat and out my mouth. We clung to each other mostly out of fear.

I was the type of woman who looked out the window and saw a parade of elephants and cats and hogs. I was the type of man who cut his food in half so many times that my bites were the size of raisins. We lived together in a hand-built structure in Vermont. We both knew conversation wasn't for us. You didn't speak for a year. Is that too long of a time not to speak?

I was the type of woman who carved local stones into ar-rows and cooked snakes into stews and looked at the sky with longing. I was the type of man who sucked juice out of straws and cooked enough grand meals to make anybody love me. We both rotted in the sand of a far-off beach. Our skin fell from our bodies and the sun bleached what was left of us until children found our remains and made them into playthings. The castles of our bones had moats, and the moon pulled the tides so close to us that water came and knocked at the door of our dead bodies. You wanted to go with the moon. I was happy to stay in the sand. What you wanted didn't matter in the end because in the end we were both taken by the sea.

BLACK TONGUE
\\\\\\\\\\\\\\\

THERE WAS A SOCKET in the wall my mother told me not to touch. The wire innards of the plug spilled out of the unguarded hole. The wires looked like black spaghetti. When my mother left the room, I walked over to the socket and bent my small body down so that my head was level with the wire mess. I inched close to the wall and closed my eyes and stuck out my tongue. My brother, who was older, once told me that one of our cousins got his tongue stuck licking a pole in winter. When my tongue licked the wires, I thought, spaghetti. When my tongue burnt black, I pulled it back into my mouth and pulled both hands to my chin. Things are so easy to ruin, I remember thinking. I remember thinking, why did I do this thing that I knew was going to have a bad ending?

LITTLE DRIPS OF WHITE PUS came out of my ears and my nails all felt as if they had been lifted off my fingers. There was an absent, lackluster silence. I couldn't hear. I wandered around the backyard and went to the shed where I kept my treasure. I dug up the box and opened it. Inside the box was a mirror.

MUCH LATER, when I was an adult, I played a sport that required one to break a lot of fingers. The two smallest sets of fingers were the ones that got broken the most. The bones are too tiny to set, all the doctors told us, so just brace them with the other, nonbroken fingers and bathe them in ice at night. The result was me having hands that looked like paddles. I wrapped the broken digits to the good ones with white waterproof tape. I imagine now, a decade after the finger breaking, that if someone were to cut open my fingers and peel back the skin, the bone would be shattered-fissured like the way rivers snake around in valleys on maps. I can still feel the cracks when I make fists.

THE SUMMER OF THE BLACK TONGUE was the summer my parents were building a new home for us. We, the children, were young, still, young enough that our parents didn't think it would matter much if we had to move schools. The parents bought a single-story rancher an hour outside of the city. We moved into the rancher and they lifted off the roof the week after we moved in. I slept on an air mattress in my would-be bedroom. If it was supposed to rain, my father got up on a ladder and put big blue tarps over all the rooms. The tarps made everybody look like they were underwater. Most nights, though, it was just stars and birdcalls. We're doing a live-in remodel, our mother told us. This live-in remodel was maybe the most fun thing we had ever done. It was like a permanent camping trip, only with better food. Most rules seemed to be forgotten. And everyone was so much nicer to one another because we were building something together. We could see the house grow day by day, mushroom out with my father's new electric saw and the new kitchen he was building in the back. It felt like the house would keep growing if I willed it. I never wanted the live-in remodel to end. I wanted everything in my life to be live-in. I wanted to do a live-in basketball game and live-in birthday parties and live-in Marco Polo with live-in friends. Can we do live-in friends? I asked my mother. That's called a commune, she said. When you're old enough, you can do live-in friends.

MY BLACK TONGUE grew into a giant slug, the kind you find in the ocean that have white dots on their backs and slippery skin. It no longer fit in the confines of my mouth so I opened my lips and let it hang out. The bigger my tongue got, the smaller my airhole was. My throat felt like the cave Jesus was left for dead in, the one whose entryway had a giant rolling rock. Don't let the rock roll over the opening, I remember thinking, keep breathing. I lay down in the shed and put two fingers in my mouth. I pressed my fingers to the top of my tongue. I felt the air go in and out of me and pictured myself from above, deflated and wrinkly.

I HAVE ONLY BEEN in one serious car crash. I was driving on the highway when it started to rain. Traffic bottlenecked and went from seventy to zero. I stopped my car along the ribbon of red brake lights. And then I saw the car from behind coming for me. I could see it the rearview mirror. He's coming, I thought, he's still coming, he's coming so fast for me, where is my body going to go? My body went forward, significantly, and then the air bag knocked me out cold. I came to bathed in my own blood. It was still seeping out my nose and onto to the white balloon in front of me when I heard the rain coming through the broken windshield and landing on top of my head.

MY BROTHER HAS ALWAYS BEEN bad with blood. When his wife birthed their daughter, he passed out as soon as the stuff started gushing out of her. People say it's like that with men, that it's not that uncommon, that even something less blood-violent than birth is liable to irk them.

People say it's because women are so used to bleeding that they're better with it, better at understanding what is at play when one's own liquid leaks. I don't think this is the case with my brother. I think he just never thinks about all the things that can go wrong. As in, there are the types of people who constantly envision what it would be like to be beheaded, and there are those who don't. My brother is the latter. He is very satisfied with his veins and the work they do to keep his blood within him. He never thinks about what would happen if they exploded and it all went wrong.

THE BUMPS ON THE TOP of my tongue looked like white pimples. I examined them in the mirror of my treasure box and squeezed to see if they would pop. Watery blood leaked out onto my fingertips. The red was only there for an instant and then it seeped into the black.

WHEN I REALIZED MY TONGUE was continuing to grow, I knew I had to tell my mother. I walked back into the house, found her working on setting some tile in one of the would-be bathrooms, and stuck out my tongue. What did you swallow, she screamed at me, what have you done?

IT IS DIFFICULT FOR ME to reconcile two of my tendencies: I have a great fear of diving boards and yet when I am on high-up platforms, such as roofs or cliff trails, I have an impulse to jump. I feel it in my feet, this kind of airy giddiness that goes what-if, what-if. Whereas, up on the diving board there is the certainty of the outcome and I clam up. I've been made to go up that long ladder by peer pressure and then there I am. I famously as a teenager actually turned around once and retreated from a high-dive, an unspeakable, shameful act at that age, so why do I have such an urge to jump off other things? Is it because the outcome is unknowable? What does my brain think I am going to do—fly? It's ridiculous that my body says, just jump off it. When I lived in a big-city apartment building and was smoking a cigarette with a friend up on the roof, I once confessed this to them and the friend said, oh, of course, me too. It's a strange feeling, the friend said, wanting to fling yourself off things. Is this why we are friends? I asked her, because we both want to jump?

IN THE CAR ON THE WAY to the doctor my mother said, oh, when I get my hands on your brother. I couldn't speak because of my black tongue. If I had been able to speak I would have told her, it wasn't him. He didn't threaten or dare or make false promises of riches. He didn't push my head down into the wires or tell me that if I did it I would gain eternal life. I did wonder at the time if this experience would make me live longer or make me more conductive. You hear stories about people who are, by no coincidence, struck by lightning twice. I did this to myself, I wanted to tell my mother. I don't know why I did this. Your guess is as good as mine.

THERE ARE GOOD THINGS ABOUT having the impulse to throw yourself off the side of a cliff. I think it makes you more likely to survive. If things get bad, I'll just learn Arabic and move to Beirut, I have thought before. If my relationship falls apart, I'll just move to Bangladesh. Surely there I can make myself again, make myself new. Maybe that's what I thought was going to happen when I stuck my tongue in. Maybe I thought it would let me start over and be reformed.

IN THE AMBULANCE after the car crash I remember putting my fingers in my mouth and feeling my tongue, all around it, underneath it and on its sides. It felt normal-sized. What was I feeling for at the back of my throat? Some type of closing? The threat of it all lurking back there deep in the depths of my mouth?

IN THE PEDIATRICS WARD my mother said, only you would do this to me. What have I done to make you do this to me? My black tongue hung out of my lips. A doctor came and put a clear moist bandage on it. Wrapped in the doctor's swaddling cloth the black tongue looked like a piece of shellacked rotten fish. Through the bandage the doctor put a needle. It felt like he was sucking out the black tongue's extra blood. Deflating, I thought again, important things are leaving me. How important is it to keep things like blood inside?

FOR MY BROTHER'S THIRTIETH BIRTHDAY, I had him and his wife over and made squid ink spaghetti. Not from scratch—I just bought it at the store. My brother was very skeptical of the color of the noodles. He was the type of kid who, for a long time, only ate things that were white and starch. Why did you make me this weird thing? my brother said after the meal was done. Why didn't you just make something I like? What happened—you went to the grocery store and you jumped in the wrong food aisle? Just because something is on the shelves doesn't mean that it's for you to try?

IN THE BROKEN-FINGER DAYS I did a lot of punching. It was all above water, legal hitting, but it was still very violent and I would, oftentimes, cause people to bleed. I crushed noses like cherry tomatoes. I made black eyes turn purple, then yellow. I was running miles a day, eating like a maniac, because no matter how much food I put in my body, I could not equal the amount of energy that left through my hits. Over the couple years I was heavy hitting, parts of my tongue got taken off while fighting. Some nut would get me hard in the cheek and my jaw would clamp quick before I got a chance to get my tongue back inside my teeth. They were just little chips, for the most part. It always felt like they more or less grew back. Whenever this happened, I'd swish my bloody tongue bits around my mouth and then, before the next throw, spit into the glove of my left hand.

THERE IS ONLY SO MUCH of your body you can ruin.

I BEND DOWN ON MY KNEES and look into the hole. In the hole I see my parents' roofless rancher and my brother playing pick-up-sticks by himself in the backyard. My mother is wearing blue jeans and a flannel shirt. She is humming to herself, scrubbing at something. She's upright and at the kitchen counter, sponge in hand. I crawl up on a chair next to her. Dinner, says my mother and my brother rushes in. Wild rice, my mother says, nothing more. Nothing more? my brother and I exclaim in unison. My mother, unfaltering, shovels the spoonfuls of it into our mouths. I choke on the rice and spit it out. My brother guzzles it down and inhales.

THE SUMMER OF THE BLACK TONGUE didn't tame me. It made me wilder, in some ways, more willing to try things because I had done the worst and survived. Yes, my mother was mad at me for a day or so, but eventually, during the afternoon of the next day, she gave in. I think the live-in nature of the whole thing made the forgiveness come faster. I was a child in a half-built house—what did she expect? I had a summer birthday, so we ended up having to do a black tongue celebration. Although the black only lasted a month or so, in the family mythology the black stuck around the whole year. The summer of the black tongue turned into the black tongue birthday, which turned into the year my tongue was colored black. My father framed a photo of me from that birthday, shirtless in our brown backyard with a stick in my hand and my tongue out, not even trying to blow out the candles, not even trying to please. Look, I was saying to the photographer, who was probably my mother, look what I've done. I have a black tongue. I won't do anything you ask of me unless I get to take off my shirt and do live-in friends.

WHEN I LOOK CLOSELY at my tongue I can tell it's actually a forest of flesh-colored flaps, small and floppy, that comb down flat when I pull them across my upper teeth. You have to brush it, my mother says. I'll have this tongue until I ruin it. Zing, I think as I stick it out, spark sizzle black.

BURN
\\\\\\\\\\\\\\\\\\\\\\\

PEOPLE KEPT DYING and I was made to sleep in their beds. The dead had been removed, and so I slept with their wives. The first to die was my neighbor, Billy Green. Billy Green had a wife named Wanda. Wanda had large breasts and hip-hugger jeans. They took Billy away in the night. I got a note on my door the next morning. It said:

> *Last night Billy Green drove his truck into a tree on Arizona Street. Wanda is now all alone. Will you sleep over at her place tonight? Keep her company at home? Make sure the shock of it all isn't too bad?*

I replied in the affirmative. I'm your man, I said. I'll take care of Wanda. I've always had a knack with cooking, and so I figured I could feed Wanda's grief. I planned to bring her some rosemary chicken and sage-butter biscuits. Maybe some lemon bars for dessert and some sweet tea for drinking. I wanted to bring her anything that would help with the forgetting, something good enough and rich enough that all her thoughts would go to her taste buds instead of into mourning.

In the evening I walked over to Wanda's and wrapped my arms around her. There was a gaggle of women weeping with her on the porch. I showed the women the food and told them to drink some iced tea and eat the lemon bars. After the women were fed and their tears turned to sniffling, I waved each one of them off into the night and said:

"See you at the service!"

"May the Lord be with you tonight!"

"Take a drink for Billy!"

They nodded and embraced me and said yes, of course, yes, we will do it all. I ushered Wanda back inside. She had the look of a squirrel who had just discovered winter. I poured her a cold cup of water. We sat in the living room. Wanda said:

"You know, Joe Engel, I just never thought it was going to get this bad. I just never thought Billy would be so nothing that he left. He left me, Joe. He put himself in that tree out of spite. I can see him in the driver's seat of the Chevy, thinking Wanda, Goddammit, I am bored as hell. You, Wanda Green, have put me here in this damn tree. I am going to lodge myself in this here trunk and make you pull me out. I am going to make you get blood on your hands and brains on your jeans and—"

I interrupted:

"That's not true, Wanda. Don't say it, because it's not true. Billy is a dead man and he didn't say any of that. The only thing he was thinking when his head hit that tree is whiskey. Let's go to bed, Wanda. It's too much. I'll sleep on the couch here, and we'll just go to bed."

"Oh, Joe, please. I can't bear to be in that room by myself. Just come and lie next to me, will you? We'll sleep with our clothes on and everything. I'm so tired, I was going to fall asleep with my clothes on, anyway. Just don't leave me alone like this."

"OK. Wanda, OK. I'll come in after you've adjusted yourself."

I could hear her in the bedroom sniffling and putting her head on the pillow. I heard her turn once and then entered after her. Sure enough, there Wanda was, in her jeans and tank top, sleeping hard. The bedroom had fake wood paneling and a large glass door that opened onto the backyard. There was a dresser and on top of the dresser was a picture of Wanda and Billy at a lake in a heart-shaped picture frame. Billy looked like he was losing hair and had somehow burnt his nose. I took off my hat and put it on the dresser and crawled into bed with Wanda. I found the groove of Billy's body in the bed frame and sunk in. I curled my knees how he had curled his. I shouldered the pillow with the same awkward angle. I heard Wanda breathe at my back as he had no doubt heard her do. The wind whispered in through her nostrils and gasped out through her mouth. Her body shuddered with life as if she was crying in her sleep. The moon came in through the sliding glass door and lightened us both. I dozed off and then woke back up sweating rain. I was so hot that my head felt pushed, cornered into a box and pressed on. I got up and got some water and took off my flannel shirt. I had an undershirt on beneath, so I figured I was still within the range of reasonable. As I was walking back to the bed, I heard a tap on the sliding glass door.

"Hey you! Joe Engel! What the hell are you doing in that Goddamn bedroom with my Goddamn wife?"

There Billy was, wispy and a bit see-through to be sure, but hollering and drunk all the same. I put a finger up signaling, "Give me a moment, Billy. Let me go get something and then I'll come outside and explain the whole thing."

He kept screaming and yelling and kicking the door. I was scared as hell Wanda would wake up and die of fright, but she kept snoring and even turned over to face the other way. I had seen a rope out in the garage earlier when the gaggle had been gathering and went to retrieve it. I put my boots back on but kept my over shirt off and put the rope over one shoulder before I slid the glass door open to meet dead Billy Green.

Billy said, "Joe. I don't know what you think you are doing in there, but that is my wife and I don't care how drunk you think I am, I am not drunk enough to look at you sleeping in my bed! I am going to beat you with this bottle and put this here dagger right through your heart!"

I let Billy say and do as he wanted because I knew his

bottle and his dagger was just smoke and air. I said, "You go ahead and try that and see how that works out for you."

I could almost see his face turning red with rage. He raised his bottle of ghost Beam and brought it down on my crown. It went straight through me. Ghost glass. It's like having a cup of cold water thrown on you, nothing more. I took advantage of his surprise and pulled his legs out from under him. I folded him into quarters and then halved him again and stuffed him in a nearby bucket. Then I took a tarp and pulled it tight over the top. Billy was sounding all muffled inside and kept hollering about his bottle. I whipped out the rope and swung it around the top and then crossed it over the bottom and tied it so tight I knew he would never get out. Then I dug a hole deep enough to stand in and placed the ghost of Billy Green at the very bottom.

"Goodbye, Billy," I said as I heaped dirt on top of the canned preserves of his soul.

Inside Wanda was still snoring. She looked pretty in this late light of the moon. I crawled back in beside her and went straight to sleeping and woke up the next morning in the most peaceful state. She made me coffee and cried a little bit, but it was a relaxed sob, not one filled with desperation. Just an exhale of air accompanied by a slow tear. After she let it out she smiled and sat down and pushed her bangs off her forehead and looked over at me.

"Thanks for staying, Joe," she said.

"Well, you're so welcome, Wanda. I wouldn't have let it be any other way."

"I heard you doing battle with Billy last night, and I want to thank you for that, too."

"Of course, Wanda. Let me know if there is anything else I can do to help."

And with that I kind of half bowed and walked out the front door and went back home to make myself some breakfast. I left Wanda the remains of the chicken and the biscuits.

As fall took hold, Wanda turned from teary-eyed to tough. I saw her at the grocery store picking out produce with the confidence of a woman who knew what she needed. In our nook of town the leaves kept turning until they twisted themselves off. Snow spattered our walkways and I shoveled what I could. It was when we were knee-deep in winter that I got another note on my door. It said:

Joe. Robert's dead. Keeled over while gardening. It is a very bad scene over here at Mary's. Come if you can. We need all the help we can get.

I stopped what I was doing and prepared myself for the white world. I got to Mary's with a thermos of hot chocolate and some coffee cake and a goat cheese–zucchini casserole and asked her if there was anything I could do. People had been over earlier, but had all left because of the early setting of the sun. Things needed to be done before the night froze. Mary didn't say anything or look up into my face. She just sat there in her easy chair, looking like she was having a vision, dry-eyed, staring off into the far corner of the room. As the night got deeper I said, "Well

Mary, time for me to get home," but then she turned and gave me this look of absolute terror so I reneged and said, "but I can of course stay if you want." She nodded her head but still didn't speak. When it got to be eleven I tried again, "Look Mary, it's late. Let's get some sleep." And in response, she held out her arms to me like a child wanting to be picked up and taken to bed. I walked over to her and she put her arms around my neck and I swung her legs under my elbow. She bowed her head in near slumber and her body bent at her torso. I carried her across the living room and down a narrow hallway filled with pictures of their wedding, their children, their generations of dogs. I pushed open the door to the bedroom with my foot and placed Mary on the side of the bed that looked like hers. I couldn't tell if she had fallen asleep in my arms or just refused to open her eyes. I made for the door, to go sleep on the living room floor, but I heard a voice behind me. At first it sounded like just a small yelp but then Mary cleared her throat and said, "Please don't." I went over to Robert's side of the bed and sat for a moment and then took off my shoes and swung my legs in. My body felt dwarfed by the imprint of his large form and the depression it had made in his sleep. Mary was breathing steady but I knew she wasn't sleeping. The snow and the walk and the carrying had tired me and despite my unease at falling asleep, I did so faster than faucet water turns cold.

It felt like I had been asleep for hours when I heard Mary's voice in the night. She said, "Ordinary man."

I said, "What Mary?"

"Ordinary man," she said.

I stayed silent and waited to see if she was going to give me more. Nothing else came.

"Mary," I said.

"Joe Engel. What are you? Are you more than you want to be, or less? What is it you are exactly? Are you how you are supposed to be? Not higher or lower but the exact fucking level that God wants you? Don't you ever think about what would happen if you stopped paying taxes? If you dyed your hair purple and got a pet hog? Is that something you would ever want, Joe Engel? It probably isn't, but don't you want to do it anyway? Do it because you can? What do you think Robert was thinking when his heart stopped while he was pulling up weeds? I bet he was like, well, fuck. I didn't even get to the rhododendrons. I mean, honestly. What kind of man thinks about the rhododendrons? Didn't he have bigger thoughts on his mind? No. No, he didn't, Joe. In fact—"

"Mary, you can stop right there," Robert said.

He was crouching in the corner of the room. He seemed to have been hiding in the closet and had slipped out while Mary had been running her rant. The midnight moon passed its light right through him and onto the foot of the bed.

"Mary. I may have kept a respectable garden, but I am not the evil you think I am."

Mary whimpered.

"Just because I grow carrots and organic grape tomatoes and beets and basil don't mean I am boring!"

"You are boring!" Mary screamed, "Even the ghost of you is boring! You aren't even *threatening.* You're just sitting there trying to convince me I should have loved you because of your Goddamn vegetable garden!"

Robert looked fairly sad. His big palms pushed into the sockets of his hollow eyes.

"Talk some sense into her, Joe," said the ghost of Robert Brown.

"Oh, no," I protested. "I'll just be on my way. Sounds like you two can figure this out on your own. No need for me to be here."

And then Mary let out a sound I honestly just did not think could come out of a human form.

"NO!" Mary sat stark up and looked like she intended to hit me with something, "Joe Engel, the only reason I even let you stay over is because I know what you did for Wanda Green! You do for me what you did for Wanda and you do it right now!"

This did not seem fair to me.

"Look, Mary," I turned to her but also tried to keep eye contact with Robert so he would feel included in the decision making process, "This seems to me like an entirely different situation. Robert is not bugging you. He is just sitting there trying to be helpful. Let him hang around awhile, won't you?"

"Joe Engel, this man has been hanging around my whole life! He is worse than a drunk, so much worse. Did you hear him talk about those damn carrots? If you don't lock him up in the ground right now I'll tell everyone you tried to get in my pants on the night of my husband's death. I will tell everyone that while I was sleeping you put your finger in my butt."

She let that sit.

"Mary!" the ghost of Robert Brown said, "Mary! How could you think such a thing, let alone say it!"

"What, Robert? You never thought of putting your finger in my butt?" Mary said, "That's right—you didn't! Maybe I wanted you to put your Goddamn finger in my butt? Maybe if you had stopped thinking about your Goddamn organic strawberries, you would have put everything where I wanted it to be put!"

Mary looked like someone had passed an electric jolt through her veins. She was standing now and her hair stood straight up and her eyes were being pulled out of her head. She menaced towards Robert. She kept yelling and walking, yelling and walking, one big terrifying step at a time. With each advance Robert dissipated. I tried to slip past the door while she was engaged with her rampage but noticed that Robert was flickering and became distracted. By the time Mary got to Robert he was gone, evaporated, no longer there.

"Where the hell is he?" Mary said, "Robert, where the fuck did you go? I have more fucking things to tell you! You fucking coward! Are you hiding in the fucking gardening shed? Oh, I'll find you!"

But Mary was alone. She had scared him right back into the afterlife. I decided to get out while I could and made my way for the front door before Mary came to the same realization. It was still snowing out and it took me considerable effort to get home. More than once in the snow I had a moment of wavering. When I got back to my house, which was bare and cold, I dried myself and bundled up and went straight to sleep.

As the days and weeks went on, I heard through the grapevine that despite the great tragedy, Mary was faring fine. I saw her at Sunday service and always offered her an extra donut, but she just scowled back. With the decrease in mature male community members, I had started taking on more responsibilities at the church. Post-service fanfare and food was a big charge, but nobody else wanted the job, or maybe there was nobody else, and I stepped in. I made lasagna and sticky buns and slow-cooked meat. When I was feeling good, I made cross-shaped sugar cookies and decorated them with red frosting to represent the blood of Christ. I wasn't sure if it was the whispers spread by Wanda and Mary or that the women just became enamored with my food, but I have had trouble with women all my life, and all of the sudden, on Sundays they swarmed around me.

"Joe, how do you get your cornbread so moist?"

"Your cookies so crisp?"

"Your pork so divine?"

And soon enough I was married. I had been a bachelor all my days, but in the thick of my life, I found myself hitched. Miranda King was her name and she had the hair of an angel, long white-blond straight hair and bangs, and she giggled when I told her how to rub a chicken. She had been once divorced, once widowed, and lived in a grand old house up on a hill. I moved in and got to cooking. I had made it through two rounds of Christmas when—*bam*— the butter got the best of me and my arteries decided half time was over. The program was being suspended. There would be no more need to flank a team. I don't remember being in the casket or watching the worms wiggle in through my ears. I remember being here and then not here. Savoring a cold glass of water and then being a cold glass of water.

Of course I went looking for Miranda as soon as I got my legs under me. I marched back up the hill and knocked on our front door. No one came at first, so I pressed the doorbell. Finally I heard footsteps and prepared myself for Miranda's embrace. But the person who answered the door wasn't Miranda. It was the ghost of Nick King.

"What the hell, Nick! What are you doing in my house?" I said.

"This is my house, in case you haven't noticed. And I have been here all along," he looked smug.

"Nick, now I realize it must have been hard dying so young and all, but Miranda and me, we have made a life for ourselves, and I think I have a right to see her and tell her I am still here."

"This house isn't big enough for the both of us," said the ghost of Nick King.

"What the hell, Nick! Where did you come from? Did my dying wake you up? Why do you think after all these years Miranda even wants you back?"

"Because I never left," Nick said. "I have been in the attic. She comes and visits me on Sundays when you are cooking. Miranda and I, we had an arrangement. You were merely fulfilling her worldly needs."

I reeled. My ghost body turned frigid and I shivered. I became disoriented and walked through a couple planters and cursed Nick and my cloud of a soul.

"Fucking Nick King! I am going to haunt you! It ain't right!" I said.

"You do that, Joe. I am pretty sure that I have been the one doing the haunting."

I tried to push him, but when my fist hit his cheek, it just went straight through. He tried to push me back, and pretty soon we were wailing and flailing without going anywhere because neither of us could get the resistance we needed. We were like two waves going through each other, two tides briefly meeting and then receding and meeting again and it appeared that this movement would go on forever, seeing as neither of our nonworldly bodies were likely to tire out any time soon.

"Joe!" we heard Miranda say, "Joe and Nick, you stop that right now!"

Miranda appeared in the living room from behind the door. I let go of Nick's collar and straightened myself out. There Miranda was, beautiful and alive and elegant and angel-faced. Her hair shone brighter, her teeth beamed whiter than I had, in my casket days, been able to recall. She looked like the picture of grace.

"Miranda," I said, "Tell me it isn't true. Tell me I haven't been living with the ghost of Nick King!"

Miranda looked sheepish.

"These things are complicated," she said, "What's a woman to do with a phantom she don't much mind having around?"

I felt completely eclipsed.

"What did you really want me for, Miranda? If you had Nick up in that attic the whole time, why need me? Did you just want me for my body? Is that the truth? Is that all you ever wanted from me?"

I was crying now. Howling and moaning.

"Shut up, Joe." Nick said, "Your body ain't that great."

This was maybe true, and it caused me to pause.

"I love you, Joe," Miranda said, "I do. And I have liked making love with you. But—"

"What!" I said. "Tell me what's wrong with me!" I said.

"Its not what's *wrong* with you," the ghost of Nick King interjected. "It's what you *provide*."

At this point Miranda started to cry. "Oh, Joe," she said, "Joe! I always loved you for you! But your chicken pot pie! Your milk braised pork with cheese! Your apple dumplings, beef stew and pecan tart! Your lemon chicken and garlic mashed potatoes and pork-tender roast! Your meatball soup and maple date bread! And sugar cookies! Oh Joe, the sugar cookies!"

My cooking achievements lay splayed out in front of me. My mother had always said that the way to woman's heart was through her stomach, but I never thought being in the stomach would feel so bad. I saw the women I had been with and I saw the pies I had fed them and I saw the memory of me feeding Miranda a slice of cake. I saw the ghost of Nick King lying down in the attic, seeing smoke from meals he couldn't smell. I saw a bowl full of grits spilled on a table and Billy Green drinking Beam and Robert Brown all frowns. Billy and Rob closed towards my table of overturned grits and picked some up with their hands and slopped it in their mouth. I looked for Miranda, and where she had been standing behind me, but all I saw was Billy, who leaned in close and slithered in my ear, "Your slow-cooked lean is going to taste mighty fine with my ghost Beam." I pulled Billy's hand off my grits and spun looking for Wanda and Mary. All I saw was the kitchen. God's great kitchen. Piles full of fish and plentiful wine. I saw me cooking casseroles forever. Churning out biscuits and buckets full of grub. Feeding God with my fingertips. Dipping my hand in a bowl of grits. Cooking God in a pot. Facing God through my stew. Him telling me to keep stirring. Just keep stirring. Don't let the citrus sour. Whatever you do, don't let the bottom burn.

GOD'S TRUE ZOMBIES
\\\\\\\\\\\\\\\\\\\\\\

In Florida things are pastel. You can't get a cup that's bright yellow. It has to be faded. Brand-new worn out. That's the way they make things there. Sunwashed and diluted. Light, light pink sunglasses with white, white hair. A reflection of what some living, vibrant human might look like. That's how most everyone looks. Generally, real people don't live in Florida. Just ghosts who are being held in Limbo for punishment of gluttony or for charging interest on loans.

Lula May
When the dead give birth to children, things split open and rip off, and it can be very expensive to replace, especially

if you want it done by a good surgeon. When Lula May gave birth, she was already dead, but her child, to most everyone's surprise, was living. A living child in Florida, her doctor said, now that's an unnatural thing. What shall he do, the doctor asked, how ever do you expect to raise a living child among those who have already passed? Many of Lula's neighbors thought the child should be sent away immediately. Put him up for adoption in a nice living state, like New Hampshire, they all said. Give the child a chance at a normal upbringing. But every time Lula considered such a thing, she realized just how much of an impossibility it was. She and her husband had never had any children while they had been alive, and now, due to some phenomena, here they were in Limbo, in Florida, with a child they could finally love and watch grow. They decided to name the child Austin. Austin Monty. And with all the love Lula May Monty's lifeless heart could muster, she clung to that child. Raised him and reared him, watched him grow hair and grow up. She would look at him going dancing with dead girls from across the street. She would smile, her smile creasing with the plasticity of her decaying face. When Austin was old enough to go out on the town, Lula May worried that the days were shortening before Austin would have to leave Florida to go be with his own. Sometimes, Austin would look at his mother, at her wild white hair, her tattooed eye liner, her gradually rotting flesh, and he would kiss her on the check, feeling the give of the skin below, wondering where his mother's body would move to next, and knowing it would be a place very different from where he was heading, a place where either things were burned and never buried, or a place where light ran wild and clouds were solid. He liked to dream of his mother and father bouncing in between God's hopping stones, leaping from one rain cloud to another. But truth be told, he wasn't exactly sure where they were destined to go. Either option, he thought, sounded better than up north.

Cassadaga

Cassadaga's vibrations reach for miles beyond its city limits; all of the mediums' psychic powers emanating out of their homes, beams of light escaping through the cracks under their doors and the spaces between their curtains. Sometimes at night, Austin would see a little stream of photons bounce around his room, knowing that there was only one place from which they could have come. Boasting the largest community of the living in Florida, Cassadaga also contains the largest number of psychics per square mile in the world. The city of seers and palms, tealeaves and chakras, meditation and communication. Come, let me look into you and tell you. Some people who visit Cassadaga are dissatisfied with the results, but naturally no one can control the spirit world. The dead are more unpredictable than the living, and often less inclined to oblige you with reasonability. In peak months, Cassadaga becomes very crowded, and with all the minds floating about, it's hard to tell whose is whose. When the mediums sleep, they unlock their skulls and let their brains float up out of their heads like balloons, their spinal cords stretching like rubber bands out of their backs, anchoring the brains to their respective owners. Sometimes, if you come to Cassadaga late at night, you can see the brains floating out of the chimneys, bobbing in the light humid breeze, sweating, slightly, because of the crowd of souls that surround them, invisibly petting and plying the mediums' brains to wake. Before Austin left Florida to head up north, his mother would take him to Cassadaga to get him used to being around living people. Austin would walk up to a medium and ask, may I touch you? My mother says it's good practice. And he would feel around their arms and their skulls, sometimes happening upon the latch that unlocked their brains (We must warn you, they would say, that not all people up north have skull latches). But the mediums were often more interested in touching him than he was in touching them. A living child in Florida, they would ponder, is it possible that he's truly alive? Or is he maybe dead and alive at the same time? Can he communicate with the spirits who have already left Florida for the next worlds? They would corner him: Tell us Austin, who do you like making love to better? The living or the dead? And Austin would blush with vivacity and reply that he had never made love to a living girl before, but that he liked dead girls very much.

The Tampa Room

The first time Austin took me to Florida, he took me to visit his grandparents in Tampa. Watch, he said to me, how the memories of the old stabilize like crystals, completely solid and unchangeable. Watch how the bungalow porches and the beach towels collage themselves into a single image, double-exposing both the past and the present, creating the illusion that time is both greater and less severe at the same time. His grandparents lived in a small, Easter-blue house. Inside the house there was a room that reeked of formaldehyde. Everything was goo and gave a little when I touched it. The photographs, the china, the pink flamingo wallpaper, the disco couches—they smelled of decay and were all slightly more pliable than they should have been. Just bending, soaked so heavy in memories that their physical substance could barely sustain the weight of their existence. On the couch a couple sat, hand in hand, jaws open, in many ways combining and exchanging substance with the couch, molding into a single, preserved entity. Gravity had taken their skin and dealt with it, and their brains were slowly dripping out of their noses and onto their shirts.

Gator Tacos

Try one, he said. It might taste like chicken, but really it's dinosaur. Not a bird, no, the other kind that somehow survived that giant asteroid that hit the earth 65 million years ago. The animal that represents the ultimate undead. He called them God's true zombies. Somehow all their relatives were massacred, and they hid under the couch and survived, thrusting their ancient, prehistoric-looking bodies into modernity. Just swaggering with scales and claws, popping out eggs that won't grow up to fly, destined to be the mascots of the modern Neanderthal, the Florida football fan. They wallow in the river and in the swamp and breathe moss onto the trees, sucking out the remaining color of the people who are still alive, diluting the air with their reptilian breath, fading vibrancy with humidity, turning the world pastel. Waddle, waddle, they slide in between the river sludge and the fan boats. Austin says to escape them you have to zig-zag. They'll never catch you if you run like a goon. Just act like an idiot, he says. That saves most people.

On Exotic Lovers

Loving a Floridian is like loving Frank Sinatra. Though he might be handsome, he is dead, so really my love is confined to a kind of removed admiration. A sulky, beaten kind of love that floats in between two people but never really sticks to anything solid. It wafts and travels between realms but, ultimately, it can never translate substance for substance—because what does an upbringing with syrupy drawls and overcrowded artificial beaches have to say to the upbringing of reality? The unease of the unfamiliar, however, is undeniably sexy, forcing my mind to jump realms into a place I have only seen in pictures and pornos. Knowing that when our mouths meet, his mouth has been in all sorts of places before mine. Florida places. In alligator swamps and in theme parks and in faded-looking ice cream shops. His mouth has been in Cuban sandwiches and in girls with bleached blonde hair, on river boats and in towns filled with psychics. On his grandparents' formaldehyde foreheads and in zombies' flesh. It is because Floridians are free of the bitterness that comes with stark definition that one can only love a Floridian if one accepts their utter separation from the rest of the world, their otherworldly upbringing that has made them so divergent from the standard color wheel, their dilution that stands so stark in the face of living flesh.

On the Mons Venus

Before Austin moved out of Florida to the land of the living, he dated a dead girl who was a stripper. She worked at the world-famous Mons Venus. At the Mons, everything yellows like a faded photograph, like a set of weeks-old unbrushed teeth. At the Mons Venus, people smash their skulls against the table to see what's inside. All the insides fall out and there are gutters on the counters to drain the contents away. At the Mons, there is a VIP room shaped like a UFO that you have to go up a tiny, tiny winding staircase to access. Once inside, there are purple plush seats and a large draining facility for people to suck out their brains. If you pay the Mons enough, they'll fill your brain with pocket-size strippers. They usually insert them through a hole they make in the very center of your forehead. They dance in your brain, puncturing your spinal column with their clear heels and their yellow teeth. Gnawing with their fingernails against the shag rug of your frontal lobes. Dancing, dancing till the rest of the plastic lining your brain cracks under the weight of their tiny feet, splintering into the bloodstream, and God decides it's time for you to leave Florida, it's time for you to go home.

WHAT I WOULD BE
IF I WASN'T WHAT I AM
\\\\\\\\\\\\\\\\\\\\

I HAD A HUSBAND. He was alive and I was yelling at him from upstairs, yelling downstairs, yelling, Ray! I can't find them! They're not here! And my husband did not answer, which annoyed me, because he frequently did not answer my questions or my calls in the way that the people you spend the most time around often do not feel obliged to do. I yelled down the stairs some more, and then I walked down the stairs and I saw him, with his head kind of bent to the side on his left shoulder and his legs straight and turned out and his arms draped over the sides of the easy chair as if the easy chair were a piece of clothing and he was wearing it like a cape. His eyes were closed and his mouth was slack. I walked up to him and yelled at him, which is when I realized that there was another reason he was not answering me, and so I shook him, which did nothing but move him, slightly. He was a big man, with big hands and freckles all across his face, and some white hair left on the top of his head. He was very handsome. I stood right next to him and I screamed at him. And then I got to the phone and called 911. The ambulance came very quickly. The medics broke down the door because I did not have the wherewithal to get up to let them in. They attached machines to my husband and counted backwards from three and the volts from the machine shook my husband and made his fingers stretch out into a perfect individualized ten, like he was reaching for something, like he was reaching for me. The medics, who had taken off my husband's clothes and electrocuted him with their machines said, I am sorry, ma'am, there is nothing else we can do, and they put my husband on a stretcher and made to take him out the door, out our door, away from me, but I said wait, wait one moment, I want to say good-bye. And so I went over to the corpse of my husband and I looked at him, and I slapped him, and said, how dare you, how dare you leave me like this, all alone.

IN A VAST WHITE ROOM that was filled with charts and fake plants, a man in a cheap lab coat who looked very convinced of his own authority held out his fist to me. He said, your husband's heart went like this, and he clenched his fist and then released his fingers from his palm and let them hang in the air and dangle. My husband's heart

wasn't made out of fingers, I said, which did not please the
doctor. It's a metaphor, he said, a visual aid to help you
understand what happened. I don't need your help, I said,
and I walked out of the white room and into the parking
lot to look for my son.

IN THE SUMMER OF 1984 my husband and I went on a
cruise in the Mediterranean that was supposed to trace
the path of Odysseus. That's how they pitched it to us.
We went with friends, three other couples, couples we had
known for a very long time. One of the funny things about
being married, especially about being married in our in-
sular, picnicking, block-partying, well-exercised group of
friends was that people were made to pretend that each
couple was one person, like most people were, in fact, only
half of one person that only became whole when paired
with a mate. We had no single friends. We went on the
cruise with the couples. I liked most of the husbands more
than the wives and everyone liked my husband more than
they liked me. It was alright that way. I am aware that I
am not very likable. I am troubled, however, by how much
easier it was for me to be with the husbands, how much
easier it is for me to talk with men. Were the women on the
cruise my husband's friends? Or were they my friends? Or
were they only friends with us as a couple? Friends with
only the double human unit we made whole? Maybe the
couples were friends with the idea of us, the idea of Ray
and Fran. In any case, it was the idea of Ray and Fran that
went on the cruise with the couples. The only interesting parts of the cruise were when the idea deviated, when

Ray and I went swimming by ourselves off the side of the ship and were left on shore for a night, by accident. What a happy accident! We were ourselves, instead of a couple, when we were alone.

I FOUND MY SON in the hospital basement, where they kept the bodies. He was looking at the body. When I got to the basement the man who oversaw the bodies said, in a very soft tone, you may want to call those who your husband was close to so they can come and see the body and gain a sense of closure. I didn't say anything back to the basement-morgue man, because I was tired, and because I have never felt particularly obligated to converse with anyone, regardless of whether or not they have already initiated a conversation with me. I did not call anyone to let them know that they could come see the body. My son was there, which was enough. Besides, my husband's body was mine, and while it was still around, albeit free of animation, I did not want to have to share it. There are so few things you can be convinced are yours. I stayed there late looking at his face. I became worried that I was letting him decompose, that keeping his filing cabinet open that long was going to crash the whole refrigerator. My husband was not old. He was seventy years old. And I was sixty-three.

I WALKED AROUND MY HOUSE, but could not look at the place where my husband had died and then found I was averting my eyes everywhere and that I could not look at anything. His death expanded from his chair to the carpets on the floor to the wood walls and the ceramic bowls in my cupboard. I looked into my bowl of cereal and I saw my husband. I looked into the grout in between my tile in our shower and I saw his hands. I heard him yelling from upstairs. I heard him yelling from outside. I started sleeping in a different bedroom, but that too became infected with him. I told my son I had to move, so he helped me find a smaller place, a duplex where I shared a wall with a young family so that I could hear people living on the other side of our shared barrier all day long and well into the night.

I DID NOT THROW my husband a funeral. I threw him a party. We burned his body and put it in a little box that I later sprinkled on the hills of a mountain where we used to hike. At the party people said, Franny, we'll miss him, we miss him so much already. The couples from the cruise came and bowed their shoulders in unison and shook their sorry heads from left to right. They had handkerchiefs. All I could think about when I saw them were the handkerchiefs. Were they old? Or had they been bought especially for that night? We were getting to an age when people were going to begin to start dying. Perhaps the handkerchiefs were an investment. Perhaps the wives had gone to the department store and bought new ones and thought, quality over quantity, we are getting to that age, it's a good investment because we will use them again.

WHEN MY HUSBAND DIED, I was so very young.

WE WERE BUILDING OUR HOUSE, Ray and I. We were going to build a house with our own hands. I was twenty-one and wore worn jeans and a black top that I had cut the collar out of so everyone could get a better view of my neck. You have to know what your strong points are, and then exploit them. I cut out all my collars. I had short dark hair that, if I wasn't so slight, would have made me look like a man. I lifted stepping stones out of a truck bed and put them in a pile on the ground. Then I called over to Ray. I said, Ray, honey love, where should we put this here path? Ray smiled very widely and walked over to me from where he had been carpentering and got very close so that all I could see of him was his chest, and he took one of his big hands and with it gripped the back of my neck and took his mouth to my ear and whispered, Oh, Franny, I really don't care. I didn't exactly smile, but kind of made my eyes bigger than they usually were and lifted the right side of my mouth and then kissed him on his chest and walked away. I laid the granite stepping stones from the driveway to the would-be front door and then there were some extra left over, so I laid some down from the backyard into the wilderness that encircled the plot of land that would become our home.

WHEN WE FINISHED building the house, it was beautiful. It was a single-level ranch-style structure with a modern single-side slanted roof and a black-bottomed pool out back that was in an organic shape, a kind of wonky oval. It was the early 1960s and I have always liked color, so I decorated the house in bright Scandinavian prints and long grotesque shag rugs. Ray had, of course, hired laborers, people he picked up at the local gardening store, to help him build the structure, but we had mostly done it alone with the help of an architect friend whom we never, surprisingly, saw much after we finished the house. It didn't seem that radical, at the time, to try and build something ourselves, something we could live in and maybe have a child in and call our home. My son insists that now it would be a clear social marker, a sign that we had certain beliefs that were not compatible with the rest of society and that we were intentionally removing ourselves from society with walls. It wasn't like that. The building of the house was Ray's idea. It was just a thing that seemed we might be able to do on our own, and why would Ray keep working his salesman job in the city when he could save money and build his own home and spend more time with me? It just seemed logical. It was like the choice to stay home with my son instead of hiring a sitter. If you like spending time with a child, and you don't have money to spare anyway, why outsource labor that you enjoy? The summer we started building, we got the frame up quick and then put a tarp over the would-be living room and lived in it like a tent. We had a camper grill that ran on small canisters of gasoline and every morning we would wake up with the sun, and shower nude with the hose and then make coffee and eat something and get to work.

Ray had a radio with which we listened to the local jazz station and memorized all the DJs' names and by the end of the summer we were doing impersonations of Billy Drake and Bobby Dale and Sly Stone when we bought groceries. We'd take our beat-up station wagon to the Safeway down in South City and I'd be in the canned goods aisle with Ray and pick up some garbanzo beans and say, Slam! That's where it's at! and slap Ray on the butt a little and slide across the slick linoleum grocery store floor while seamlessly depositing the can into our modest cart of house-camp-summer supplies. We bought lots of things we didn't need on those grocery trips. We bought cereal boxes that had funny names, like Lots O Nuts and a box of Jello called Slime Pie. We ended up mixing that funny green Jello box mix with water and feeding it to the birds. They loved it. The jays and the cardinals slurped it up like ice cream soup. Look, Ray! I said. The birds love us! Ray looked at the birds and then he looked at me and laughed and said, It's a good thing I don't really like birds, because I wouldn't be surprised if that kills them. No, I said. No, look! They love it! But Ray insisted that the Slime Pie would make them die. I kept buying it and kept feeding it to the birds anyway, and the only dead jay I ever saw at our house was one that had been killed by our cat. They survived, I told Ray when the summer was done and we had our roof and most of our walls. Look at them in the trees! I said. They love me! Maybe, said Ray as he turned back to his task and tried to finish painting one of the front house panels before the last of the light closed in on our little hill and it turned dark.

AFTER RAY DIED, I lived in the duplex. I liked being able to hear the neighbor children's young feet run back and forth. I imagined the children running very fast like small dogs, and then suddenly stopping, closing their eyes and falling smack on their faces fast asleep. I will admit that there were times when I put my ear to the wall, when I slid my pressed body from the first floor to the stairs, and up them, just to follow the family's evening, to hear the father giving a bedtime story and putting his little boy and girl to sleep. I realized, after some time, that my mind was playing tricks on me. That I would hear conversations on the other side of the wall that did not exist. One day I had my head pressed to the side of the kitchen, and I heard the young husband and wife arguing about Slime Pie, why it was still on the grocery list, what a waste of money it was, and how it would surely kill the birds. My God, I thought, it's Ray and I in that apartment, and I began to cry. I became very worried that I had invented the whole family, that I was, in fact, in a regular house, not a duplex, all alone. I rushed out into the front yard to make sure the house was doubled, to make sure that there were two front doors and a wall that was shared. I looked at the duplex. It was a building folded over, and duplicated. There was certainly another structure that was connected to mine. I rang the doorbell of the other front door. A handsome young man immediately came and answered it. Fran, he said, Fran, how are you doing? Is there anything I can get you? Do you want to come inside? No, no thank you, I said. I said, I am so sorry to bother you, I thought I heard someone inside cry.

IT IS DIFFICULT FOR ME to distinguish which parts of myself are the original me, which parts of myself predated Ray, and which parts were developed while I was with him. And, for those parts of me that were developed while I was with him, how am I to tell which parts I would have developed on my own, without him, and which parts of myself never would have come to pass if I had never met him? For instance, I am a painter. I paint portraits of people, portraits of people I like, or people who I meet that interest me. I have sold some paintings for some money, and a gallery in the city, one time, even put on a full show of my work. However, I rarely show the people I paint their portraits, because I think that they would not like them, that they would be angry and insulted that I had painted them in such a way. They are not realist paintings, but they are most definitely portraits of specific people, and after I paint a portrait, it can be difficult for me to not think of the portrait as a summary of that person, which is why I have always liked painting people multiple times, because of course people change, and my understanding of people changes, so of course, over time, my portraits of specific people will be very, very different. In this way, I think of my paintings as a kind of thesis of my understanding of someone, and I can look back at all of my paintings that I have made of a specific person and see how my understanding of that person has changed. I started painting when I was a young mother, when I was twenty-four and was home all day all alone with Adrien, our infant son. While Ray was at work, I walked down the hill to a small convenience store and bought a cheap, child's set of watercolors, and then I marched back up the hill with Adrien in my arms and the package of paint tucked under my arm. I put Adrien on the floor, on one of the faded shag rugs, and ripped out some pages from a notebook and painted him. I painted a can of peaches and a spoon, and wrote under the image ADRIEN, MAY 5TH 1966. I painted him each day for a week, and then I began to paint people I saw in the grocery store. I would put Adrien in the stroller and roll him down to the store, with the paints hidden in the bottom compartment of the stroller, and stand in the frozen foods section and watch people open the icy doors, and watch the small, cold clouds slick out of them, and watch the people hover over ice cream choices and frozen vegetable dilemmas. I eventually became very friendly with the grocery store staff, in particular, one man who was about nineteen who I suspect was in love with me. His name was George and on the third day he saw me in the frozen food aisle he brought me a stool to sit on. When he gave it to me, I looked at him very gratefully. I said, thank you so much, thank you, you have no idea what this means to me. And, the next day, when I came back, I gave him some cookies which I had baked at home the night before. In this way we became friends. In between stocking the shelves and mopping up messes, he would come speak to me. And I asked about his life, where his parents lived, if he had a girl and if he was happy with his work, doing what he was doing, doing what he wanted to do. He was very happy, and happier now that I was there, he said. I got in the habit of calling the store if I knew I was going to be absent and had to be elsewhere or had to stay home. I didn't want George to worry. I wanted him to know I wanted to be there, I wanted to be in the frozen food aisle with him making my pictures, sharing an apple, talking about nothing, most of all not about Ray and my life in the house we had built with our own hands that now had a somewhat neglected front lawn and a roof that was not as structurally sound as we had planned.

I KEPT THE PORTRAITS in a large cardboard box in the hallway closet that housed the vacuum cleaner and other supplies that I couldn't dream of Ray ever wanting. Still, he found them. He brought them out one night after dinner. He said, Franny, what are these? Where did they come from? He said, Franny, these are beautiful. Did you paint these? You have a gift, you must keep on with them, and we must get you all the supplies that you need. I never, in my deepest dreams thought that my paintings were about anything other than a misunderstanding, me, as a person, being somewhat defect and not really being able to understand people unless I tried especially hard. That is all the paintings were supposed to be, a tool for helping me better process the world that was around me. And here Ray was, telling me they were beautiful! That they were worth something! That I owed it to myself and others to keep on! Ray started telling people, friends of ours, about my paintings at dinner parties. One of the neighbors suggested that we turn the backyard shed into a studio, and Ray was enthralled. He came and met George down at the

Safeway, and him and George got along so well, and Ray even hired George to do some yard work for us and invited him over for dinner, and all of a sudden the idea that I had ever been scared or ashamed of the work I was doing, the notion that I had been doing something covert and wrong, became absurd. People began to know this about me, they began to know that I made paintings, and then, all of the sudden, people introduced me as a painter and it was what I was. One of Ray's bosses came over for dinner and asked to see some of my paintings, and I brought out one of the frozen food aisle portraits where I had painted a box of frozen peas against a red wash and written underneath WOMAN IN FUR COAT AND SANDALS in cursive script. Ray's boss said it was fabulous, he loved it, is there any way he could pay me for it? Take it with him and hang it in his home? I said, absolutely not, it was a gift, he could have it, but the boss would have none of it and assured me and Ray he would pay one way or another, and he did, later that fall, when in November Ray got a corporate bonus of $1,000 that came in on his paycheck labeled FOR THE PAINTER. And so, in this way, I began to make things and people talked about me this way, as a person who made things, as a person who painted, and I liked that this was the way that I was known in our small, close-knit group of friends because it gave me a pass of some kind, where now it was all of a sudden more acceptable for me to be less likable, because I had other qualities that people seemed to think were of interest and were worth having around.

WHEN RAY FIRST TOLD ME in our living room that the paintings were good, I did not believe him. How could I believe him? I was horrified that he had found them and suspected him of making fun of me, or trying to control me in some way that I could not understand. I was very cold to him and I started to cry and said, you just leave me here all day all alone, you musn't be angry at me, please don't yell at me. Ray had never yelled at me. And I realized, later, that I was yelling at myself, that everything I feared Ray would say was something I had already said to myself in my head.

I WAS A GOOD MOTHER, although I did do things other mothers we knew didn't do, mostly just benign things like taking Adrien on long walks alone, walking him down our hill and across our suburb to somewhat deserted parts of our city, like the shipyard, where we watched people and things come and go. If he was sleeping, I'd push his stroller down our hill and across many roads until I reached the overpass where, if you turned left, there would be rows of warehouses. There was a summer, the summer when Adrien turned four, when we went to the warehouses frequently. It was the summer I mostly wore a blue sundress I made for myself and a large straw hat, and Adrien wore the same purple and green block print jumper every day. Adrien and I, we'd just sit and watch the men loading and unloading bags of rice and tiles and textiles all day long, until around three-thirty, when we would begin to walk home and I would ask him questions about the scenery as we walked. Adrien, I would say, what do you see? And, at first, of course, he only said the usual things, like, I see clouds and a tree. So then I asked him to say what he saw beyond the things he saw, like, for instance, our hill we lived on. I would ask, Adrien, what's behind our hill? And he would say wonderful things, like, a village of talking rabbits where the king rabbit has just been killed OR a beach where everyone's bathing suit is made out of goldfish. Once, on one of our long walks, I asked him, Adrien, what is behind that tree? And he said, a man, a very dirty man that has stuffed animals and sleeps in the grass, but he is hiding. And there was a real man that I had not seen, which was very scary, and was maybe one of the only times where I have ever been instinctually worried about how, if something were to happen to Adrien, other people would think of me. They would say, that woman, that Fran, that woman. She got her son butchered by the warehouses, that woman. She practically gave him to the murderer, offered Adrien, her small defenseless son up for slaughter, that's what she did. That was the thing with motherhood that caught me off-guard. I am not the type of person to really care what anyone thinks of me, but I found myself caring, very much against my will, what people thought of me as a mother. I wanted to be a good mother. I wanted people to believe I was a good mother, because I love my son very much, and, although I have always doubted my capability to do and be many things, I have always been quite sure that I knew how to properly love someone, and the idea that I might be bad at loving my son was very scary to me then, and it is, still, one of the great invisible monsters of my life that I have tried to battle, but it has always been unclear in this battle whether there ever was a battle and, if there was, whether or not I won.

WHEN ADRIEN BECAME AN ADULT, maybe two or three years after he graduated from college, it became obvious to me that he believed his father was perfect, which was of great annoyance to me. Ray was not perfect. I was frequently tempted to explain to Adrien all of his father's flaws. I wanted to tell him, you know, he may seem open-minded in some ways, but don't be fooled! The things Ray would say! You would be horrified. Here, just let me give you a list of the things I hate about my husband: his complacency. If the world suddenly turned bright blue, he would not be fazed; he would be accepting, which is completely unreasonable. He wouldn't know why it was blue, and he wouldn't care, or he would care, but only if someone told him to care, like me, like if I said, Ray! The blueness is killing the planet! Then he would say, well shoot, Fran, let's do something about it. But he would never come to that conclusion all the way on his own, so you'd have to kind of help him there, which really, after many years, makes you wonder, it makes you wonder what it would take to make him realize on his own that something was wrong. Like when Adrien was seventeen and drunk-drove his car into a tree and then walked the rest of the way home and Ray said, let's talk about it in the morning, maybe this can all be explained. No! There was nothing to explain except for what happened, a plain fact that Ray understood but could not fully, in its repercussions and possible causes, comprehend. Adrien could have killed someone, could have killed himself, but all Ray could see was that Adrien was hurt, upset, drunk. Whereas I, in that moment on our front stoop, on the welcome mat of our sagging handmade home, all I could see was a corpse, Adrien dead, an alternate history that had been so close to happening that it drove me mad. People should be driven mad, temporarily, when they see things like that, their son in a near-miss state. Sanity, Ray's level-headed gait, was completely intolerable. Which brings me to another one of Ray's flaws: his complete inability to condemn someone, even privately. I realize that the world we live in makes us, at times, have to interact with people that are less than savory, people who have different beliefs, different value systems, maybe even value systems that you know, critically, most definitely harm other people, like high-frequency traders, like oil corporation executives, like women with big diamonds hooked to their palms, what I am saying is that I realize that situations may arise in which one would have to fraternize with such company but when you get home and into the bedroom and you are free of the constraints for which politeness calls, you should be able to say to your husband, that man was awful. And your husband should say, yes, despicable, quite. Not Ray! My God, he gave the benefit of the doubt to everyone. A terrible mistake, by all accounts, a mistake that caused me to endure many unpleasant dinner guests. Eventually, with these people, Ray would slowly come around and admit they were terrible, but it took such a long time and then I was always left feel-

ing awful, like I had forced badness on this person's rep-
utation, even though this person had brought about the
badness all on their own. I told Ray this a million times,
I said, look, here is the thing with people, you can tell if
you have a really bad egg very quickly. There are many
cues by which you can discern said bad egg. And very
rarely, only very rarely, are those first-five-minute bad egg
impulses not confirmed. It is kind of like feeling humidity, I told him, it's just in the air and you feel it on your
skin. But Ray never listened to this advice. He accused me
of keeping mental judgment boxes where, once I decided
someone was a bad egg, I put a transcript of every con-
demnable thing they ever said. This accusation was not
true, I just remember when people say offensive things.
Everyone does this, I explained to him, except, obviously,
for you, who are so morally tone-deaf that I wouldn't be
surprised if you gave Lucifer a Nobel Prize. If he was in
a good mood, Ray ignored everything I said and told bad
slapstick jokes on repeat until I laughed or walked away
and cooled off and resigned myself to living with someone
who was morally deaf. If he was in a bad mood or tired,
he just let me talk at him, talk him into the ground until
there was nothing left of him. And he said nothing or, if
he was very tired, he said, Fran, I am sure you are right.
The only thing Ray never admitted I was right about was
when I told him I wanted to leave him. He said Fran, you
are wrong, how can I show you you are wrong. He kept
saying, look at how much I love you, look at it. It was very
difficult for me to look. Adrien was in high school and I
was painting on larger canvases and questioning my me-

dium, and there Ray was, stagnant, same as he always was, and I doubted him. I doubted his sincerity, but most of all I doubted his capacity to give any part of himself to me which, the longer I thought about our marriage, was what I really wanted. I wanted to have a part of him that no one else had. Ray always talked me down when I threatened to leave him, most often by physical force, the physical act of him holding me while I cried. He said, I love you, Franny, I'm just not the same as you which is why you can't see it, I can't do feelings like you, and our feelings don't look the same which is why mine are hard for you see, but they are there, Franny, you're really the only thing that ever mattered to me, you know it, I want you to know it, what can I do to make you see?

THERE WERE THINGS that made me feel very close to Ray and other things that made me feel so far from him, like we were animals of different species and the fact that we cohabitated, let alone mated, was completely bizarre. It didn't seem that way at first, of course. At first we were just kids living in the city, making money as best we could away from our parents, living in small, cramped shared apartments and watching movie matinees until we were crazy enough to pool all of our resources and buy a small plot of land fifteen miles south of town. Back then, when we found each other, it was like we were the only two people in the world, the only two people at the party, the only two people in the building, the only two people in the whole damned city, it was incredible, a feeling I suppose many people have had, but it still felt very unreal and, well, I guess I was young (I was only twenty-one), but that feeling was enough and filled everything, every space of our lives and all the cupboards and all the food we put in our mouths. There was a closeness then, but it was different from the intimacy of me trying to leave, and there was no trace yet of the bizarre, any inkling that I would ever look at him and think, how on earth have we ever been able to communicate about anything, let alone anything of importance, like our home and our life and our son.

I BEGAN TO SUSPECT THAT Ray handled me like he handled discovering my paintings, like I was just one constant discovery, a never-ending box of surprises that, when discovered, was just a new turn in the road to be taken without blinking at high speed. Which, although it sounds glamorous, was actually not a good feeling. It made me feel like my husband could be in love with anyone, like if I hired a double and put someone completely different in my place, he wouldn't even suspect that it wasn't me. He would just think, here is the newest Fran! And continue on with the meal. The only time I could ever be sure Ray knew who I was was when we were making love. He always knew exactly what I wanted, and the older we got the more I could not remember if it had always been this way, or if he had just learned my body so well, refined the act of making love to me to such a fine-tuned skill, that he was able to play my body with such unhindered dexterity. And I wondered, also, if this was the way it was with all couples that put in the hours of twenty years, if it always got to a point where, physically, pleasure became easy, the only uncomplicated thing you could count on, a set of simple, uncomplex actions, or combination of actions that, without fail, yielded great temporary joy. His body, Ray's body, was what was the realest to me. It was his body, not his mind, that I felt I was able to know in a way I will never know anything else. The body, after all, is an object that takes up physical space that one can touch and see and explore and remember and it changes, yes, but only slightly, and the changes usually make sense, as in, they can be seen as a logical progression, like how Ray's hair turned from dark to white, like how the skin on his ass was firm and, later, like mine, had elements of paper, but the body makes sense in that way, whereas the mind, Ray's mind, was unknowable, and the changes even more opaque. When we had sex, I knew I was coupling with some combination of Ray's mind and his body, but mostly I just liked thinking of us as two bodies. It was simpler that way and easier for me to understand.

THREE YEARS BEFORE RAY DIED, he retired. My father had died the year before and left us some unexpected property and cash, and by then we owned our house free and clear. So we didn't have much money, but we knew we had enough where we wouldn't run out and even a little left over so that we could take a trip once a year to a place we had read about or had just, simply, always wanted to go. Ray was most interested in the national parks, staying domestic, doing long car rides to the center of the country where we could see the great mountains and bison and rainbow trout fish. I told him that the idea of driving to Wyoming was pathetically American and that I just didn't know if I could stand it, even though, the truth was, I liked the mountains and I liked hiking and I was, in fact, very American, and the thought of seeing strange, archaic animals roam on vast plains didn't seem all that bad. We can drive when we are old and eighty! I said. Let's go on a plane! Alright, Ray said, we can go on a plane. So we agreed to save the trip to Yellowstone for later, and that summer we went to Tuscany for a month where we rented a small stone cottage on the edge of a vineyard that was once used to store barrels of wine. And the summer after that, we did the Odysseus cruise, and the summer after that we went to Sydney, and then Ray was dead and so he never saw Saddle Mountain or Republic Peak or the Needle or any of the other geological formations that he had read so much about in that small book he owned titled *The Mountains of Our National Parks.*

ONE NIGHT WHEN I WAS alone in the duplex, I watched a movie about dams, and how they were killing all the fish, and how if you wanted to see a steelhead trout, you had better come quick before they were all gone. And I thought, Ray would have loved these dumb fish, he would have talked about them with the neighbors, and known everything about them, and known where they were on the Snake River, and where they were spawning, and this movie, this would have been the catalyst if we had watched it together, this would have been the last straw, that was it! We were driving to Yellowstone for the fish and you know, you know, I would have loved it, although I might have pretended to go reluctantly just for Ray's sake, to get him to smile extra and let me pick the music for the car and so I could put my head on his lap while he drove us all the way out into the middle of our country and then home.

EVEN THOUGH I DOWNSIZED when I moved to the duplex, I still had lots of room, so I made a pottery studio in the basement and set up my painting studio upstairs. Potting was new to me but I felt I needed something new, and the idea of creating something functional, something three-dimensional that one could put sugar or flowers in, was satisfying. I made large thrown bowls with ombré glazes and rustic white square plates on which, when the couples came over for dinner, I served fruit and cheese. At one of my duplex dinner parties, one of the husbands from one of the couples said, you know, Franny, have you ever thought about doing an artist residency? It's a great way to travel, and you'd be with other people and your paintings are so gorgeous, you could have time to paint, and they are usually in beautiful places, and I bet you'd have fun. The husband who had said this was not one I particularly liked, but I had a certain respect for him, so I looked into it. One of the first residencies I found that was of interest to me was the National Park Residency Program and, sure enough, there were cabins in Yellowstone where

you could live for the summer and paint and, to my surprise, the program accepted me and I went. So, in the summer of 1989, I packed my paints and some good, practical,
outdoors outfits and I drove to Wyoming. The whole drive
there I couldn't help thinking of the fish from the movie,
frantically swimming back upstream until they hit a dam.
That was what I was sure I was going to hit when I got
there, some giant concrete wall that wouldn't let me in.
On top of the dam I saw Ray weeping, his tears hurtling
over the barrier, mixing with the rest of the river, crashing overhead faster and faster, crushing the fish, crushing me trying to get into the park. It's not that I prevented
Ray from coming to Yellowstone, that I said, oh no, I won't
do it, this is not something I want to do, I just didn't do it
with him in time, there hadn't been enough time, I hadn't
known that there wouldn't be more time. And so when I
went, when I drove into the park and rolled down my window at the ranger's checkpoint and showed them my res-
ident artist's pass I just felt this deep, deep sense of sad-
ness that I think came from being faced with the fact that
there were times when I could have done things to give
Ray happiness that I deliberately did not do. And so Yellowstone became a kind of symbol in my mind for everything Ray had wanted that I had not given him: another
child, a kind word about his mother, an evening in which I
did not chastise some of the people with whom he worked,
an evening in which I told him, Ray, I love you hopelessly,
you have become a part of me, and now I feel as though
I'll never be alone. But doing these things, saying these
things, was not, is not, how I would ever really do things,

so perhaps if I had done them, given myself up to them, Ray would have recognized their out of character nature and made me stop.

MY YELLOWSTONE CABIN SAT a small walk away from another cabin that contained another artist, a composer, a man about my age, maybe a little younger, whom I would peek out my window and see, lights on, working through the night. His name was Barclay Rowland and he requested I call him B. I asked why he had two last names and he said, good question. He was very quiet, and very slim and wiry. He looked like he knew how to hike, so I asked him if he would like to go on a hike, and on a hike we went. We became friends, and in the evening I'd invite him over for vodka and lemonade on my small front porch. Each of the artist's cabins had a rocking chair out front and, one day, finally, about a month into our three-month stay, B hiked his rocking chair all the way from his cabin to mine. He said, I am tired of sitting on the floor! I need a chair to have my vodka in! Of course we slept together. Sleeping with B, sleeping with a man other than Ray, was not what I thought it was going to be. B walked me inside my cabin and took off my collarless shirt (the strength still worked) and kissed me very softly for a very long time, too long of a time perhaps, and I began to get worried, like a teenager, that we would never get past second base. He did, eventually, put his hand in my pants and the rest was quick to follow, but it wasn't urgent, and it was a bit belabored, and I found myself, more than I wanted, looking past his shoulder, to the opposite side of the room, my mind wandering elsewhere, away from me, into some far-off space.

B AND I PARTED WAYS very amiably. He wrote frequently, at first, and said he wanted to come visit, we could have another adventure together, but I wrote back reluctantly and eventually stopped my reply. The canvases I had worked on that summer had almost all been portraits of Ray, all fourteen of them. I was evasive with B about my work, when we were together. I only showed him a couple pieces, pieces steeped in symbols that could, I knew, be taken as graphic pieces, so I never had to explain to B what they were about, what I was circling around during our summer in the woods. B asked, of course, what they meant to me, but all I said was just that they were the images I saw in my sleep, dream sequences that came to me when I was between consciousnesses. I have, since that summer with B, slept with other men. But sleeping with other men has always been a bit tricky. I think the trickiness has something to do with my problem of understanding my own identity, which parts of it are me and which parts of it were Ray, and which parts of it were me that only developed because Ray was there with me. Sleeping with these other men, B and beyond, I just can't help thinking during the act that they are fucking Ray and me, together, bringing us both pleasure, that I am somehow the physical embodiment of both myself and Ray at the same time. It's not that I feel Ray is in the room, watching me, no, I feel that Ray is inside my chest, occupying half my brain, sharing the body that is taking place in the physical act. This is especially strange because, when Ray had been alive, when I had had sex with him, I had always been sure of my body, that it was mine, that I was in it, just as sure as I had been of his. So, to be compromised this way, unsure of who exactly was in me, was alarming, although, with time, I have grown used to experiencing this feeling and it no longer inhibits me, ever, from doing anything I desire to do.

ONE OF THE ROTTEN THINGS about having a body is that you don't realize how many parts you have until they've all gone wrong. Aging has been fine, I don't mind the looks of it and in a lot of ways I appreciate being able to look the way I feel, looking very old and very tired gives you a certain edge on things. And, also, being able to look heroic. I've been told I have that look about me now and I expect that I, old woman that I am, very well should. There is part of me, though, that suspects I have always looked this stoic, and now I am just old enough where a feeling of removed superiority is an acceptable attribute to possess.

I LIVE IN A HOUSE, now, that is surrounded by other houses inhabited by other people of an advanced age and a middle-aged woman named Maria comes in the mornings to help me get dressed and take me for a walk. Adrien comes and visits frequently with his wife and their little girl and small dog and I paint the lot of them in a family portrait at least once a year. I refuse to show Adrien the paintings, which is silly, I suppose, at this point, but Adrien's wife, Ella, likes them, and makes sure they sit for me each year which makes me feel good, like I still have to do something, another year with Molly, their daughter, sitting patiently in the painting, another year where Adrien still has hair and that smile of his and his expertly placed arm. They offered to let me live with them when I admitted that I needed some help. No, I said, no. You have your lives and I have mine. I have my paintings, which as you know, I am deep in these days, and how would I get any work done with you there to distract me? Peering over my shoulder or around my side? In my home, which the staff calls Cottage 18, I do have a nice place to sit and paint. I still am drawn to painting portraits. I paint Sophia, my main nurse, and some of the other residents, like Demetri, an ex-contractor, and Gary, an ex-banker with expensive clothes. It is notable, however, that for the first time in my life, I have been moved to paint self-portraits. When I paint myself, I can feel Ray at the edges, around the back of the canvas, in between the paint and the thread, in between myself and what I really am. You hear all this talk of souls, especially in places like these, places for the elderly. They try to convince you, or they think it is comforting to hear that there is something within you that is unchanging, something that has been in you since you were born and that will live on after you die. Though I am not drawn to the idea of an unchanging essence, there does seem to be something to the idea that there are things that can change you, people who can place themselves in you and never leave. I mean, Ray's been dead for decades, enough time for a whole other life to be born and ended, enough time for someone to completely change who they are and what they see when they wake up and get out of bed and walk out of their home into the street. I don't tell Adrien this, but it still feels that there is a part of Ray in me, that he left something in me that I can't shake off. Which makes me think about what I would be if I wasn't what I am, what I would be if I wasn't just Fran. Perhaps the couples were right, those old friends that needed so badly the idea of something, the idea of Ray and Fran, to invite us on their vacations and onto their front lawns. I resented this want of theirs so badly. I was myself, and I wanted it to be known. But maybe the idea of us was always the reality, the Fran, the mother, the painter was none without Ray, her level-headed mate, and maybe that's why the self-portraits keep coming out like this, with ghosts in the corners and Jello boxes and rainbow trout fish. Or, maybe, I am truly just Fran. Ray died and left me. There is nothing of him within me. He sat down in his easy chair and closed his eyes and left through the top of his head. In that case, everything I see creep in at the edges of myself is only a wanting, only a desire to not be left with myself in Cottage 18, a desire to be more than a single person trembling, a wish to be forever coupling so that I am not just simply alone.

NAVE
\\\\\\\\\\\\\\\\\\\\\\

MY FATHER TOLD ME that our church had a belly. It was named nave and sat at the very center of the cross, in the meat where the two structural lines crossed. I never saw anyone feed the nave and feared it was hungry. When we went to church I brought it things I thought it would like. I stuffed almonds in my pockets and gummy bears in the backs of my shoes. I whispered things to the floor, sure that the nave could hear me. I said, "I know you must be hungry because all the adults bring you is money."

I pulled my profferings out and stuck them under the rug and mashed them up a bit with my foot so the nave wouldn't have to chew. I brought it raisins and cereal and sometimes even honey. I hid the food in my jacket and when the adults weren't looking, I fed the ravenous nave like my parents fed me.

I always sat in the same seat because I liked the smell of the rot the nave gave me. No other children would sit next to me, and my parents did not like that I sat alone. After several weeks the adults began to sniff and told me the place where I sat was stinky.

"I am having private time with God," I lied to them. I knew I had made the nave too dependent. I knew that if I didn't feed the nave, I would be the nave's next feed.

At home one Sunday we ran out of snacks and I threw a fit. I refused to attend church, but my mother had none of it and I was dragged out to the car, down the road, and into a new seat in a pew between my parents.

The whole mass I could hear the rumblings of the church's belly. The nave yelled and screamed. It wanted a granola bar. It wanted goldfish. It wanted all of the snacks I had ever brought it and it wanted them now.

Knowing that the time before the nave would eat me was near, I began to cry. I readied myself for the ground to open. For the thin red carpet to rip and split into a fleshy cavern filled with thousands of teeth that crescendoed from smallest to biggest, so that there were daggers at the opening and a dense white center in the bellows that circled a tiny hole where all the fluids of the masticated people were slurped down and funneled directly into the stomach of God.

ARMS OVERHEAD
\\\\\\\\\\\\\\\\\\\

MARY READ to Ainsley.

"Don't pause between the pages," Ainsley instructed. "It interrupts the story. You have to read ahead a little or slow down your speech while you're flipping, so you can say the sentence that straddles the pages without a noticeable break."

Mary read, "The ouroboros slays, weds, and impregnates itself. It is man and woman, begetting and conceiving, devouring and giving birth, active and passive, above and below at the same time."

"That's right," Ainsley said. "That makes perfect sense to me."

"Does it, though?" said Mary. "How can it mate with itself?"

"It puts its tail in its mouth, that's how."

"So, it metaphorically reproduces," said Mary.

"Don't be dense, Mary," said Ainsley. "It's science."

Mary continued to read and Ainsley continued to listen. Mary was sitting cross-legged, balanced on a stool. Ainsley was lying flat on the wood floor, limbs and hair spread all around. They were both smart girls, but were young enough and pliable enough that it was not yet clear who was smarter. They were the only two people they knew who read a significant amount of books, so they read a great deal together, but they also took long walks in the forests that surrounded their houses and, during the summers, frequently swam and sunned themselves at the community pool.

They thought of themselves as many things, but mostly as humans who other people seemed to identify as young women, which appeared to come with a great many problems, most of which they knew, but some of which they were still in the process of discovering. They had a private joke between the two of them that they were not girls, but, rather, vegetation, plants whose souls were mistakenly rerouted toward the incorrect vessels, and that is why sex made very little sense to them, and why it required a great deal of discussion. In line with their vegetal alter egos, the girls sometimes called each other Red & White, in reference to their favorite fairy tale, because Mary had the dark, tight curls like Rose Red and Ainsley had the pale, blonde, water-straight hair like Snow White. Also, they lived in a part of the country where one had to walk through the woods a great deal to get anywhere, which seemed to them how things were in the story, and they were, always, traversing the pine-needle paths to get to each other's houses, so it seemed like a good joke, but also something kind of nice to fantasize about, the two of them someday shape-shifting into flowers and ending up in the same bouquet.

"How can something be above and below at once?" said Mary

"If it's inside something else," said Ainsley.

"Oh, I see."

Mary's mother came into the living room where they had been reading. She was weathered and weary-looking in her pantsuit, her hair slicked back into a tight ponytail, her lipstick settled in between the cracks in her lips.

"What do you think it means to try and eat yourself?" Mary asked her mother.

"What would you like to eat for dinner?" Mary's mother said. Ainsley brought her knees to her chest and pushed herself off the floor. Mary got down from the stool. Ainsley and Mary followed Mary's mother into the kitchen.

In the kitchen was Mary's father and little brother and a dining table that housed a bowl of oranges. The little brother was barely old enough to chew and sat strapped in a seat that had a built-in tray for catching all the food he wasn't able to slather all over his face or insert in his mouth.

"Thank you for having me over for dinner," said Ainsley.

"I can't believe they are closing down another office," said Mary's father.

"Please, can't we talk about something else?" said Mary's mother.

"Ainsley," said Mary's father. "Are you looking forward to going back to school?"

Ainsley was not looking forward to going back to school because she had been forced to enroll in Physical Education, a class Mary was not required to take because Mary planned on participating in several group sport endeavors including soccer. Ainsley didn't like sports. Mary told Ainsley she should try something solitary, like running or swimming. It'd be better than having to sweat in between classes and change in and out of gym shorts. Ainsley, though she was dreading PE, was unsure which option would bring her more displeasure, and, stuck in a fit of indecision, had missed the deadline to sign up for any sports teams and was, therefore, automatically enrolled in PE.

"I am very much looking forward to being in high school," said Ainlsey. By which she meant, she was tired of being a child. Which wasn't totally the truth, because she suspected that she was also tired of being an adult. Whatever the case, it didn't matter, because Mary's father went back to talking about offices and what he wanted from his company, and what he thought his company wanted from him. Mary noticed the way her father talked into the air like a spore-releasing perennial. He looked at Mary's mother when he spoke, but when his words came out of his mouth they landed everywhere, all over the kitchen, in a kind of indiscriminate spray that struck Mary as very foul.

"It would be a strange thing to try and eat yourself," Ainsley said as she bit into a leg of chicken. "Just because we don't have tails doesn't mean we couldn't, obviously. I mean, it would be more of a disjointed endeavor but surely it could be done. Of course, how far you get is another question. But with the aid of drugs and things, I think you could get very far."

"It seems to me more like a metaphorical consumption," said Mary. "It's about knowing yourself, maybe? But there is violence in it too, I suppose. The idea of having the capability to destroy yourself, perhaps."

"I think it's a question we should ask ourselves. Could I eat myself? Well, like I said before, it's really just a question of how far."

Mary and Ainsley excused themselves from the table and washed their dishes. They went back to the living room where they got on the family computer, went to the town library website, and searched for and subsequently reserved several books on the subject of cannibalism.

"As roses," Ainsley joked. "Eating yourself would be super hard!"

"I guess you're right," Mary giggled. "It isn't like we'd have the convenience of mouths to put ourselves in. We'd have to somehow convert our bodies into light and then find a way to devour the sun rays."

"That sounds a lot more fun than eating yourself limb by limb," said Ainsley.

When it was 9:00 p.m., Ainsley said it was about time

she went home. Mary hugged her and walked her as far as the back porch where she waved Ainsley into the woods. Ainsley's golden-white hair hung behind her in a steady swinging. Mary's eyes followed Ainsley's illuminated locks deep into the trees.

In the morning they met at the library where they picked up their books on cannibalism. Backpacks loaded, they exited the library, walked down the front steps and turned left. The road they walked along was a thorough-fare. There were many cars that passed them on the right. As they walked, a car slowed next to them and rolled down its window. The car was filled with four or five men, who looked like they were all about twenty years old. One of the young men stuck his head out the window and yelled something at Mary and Ainsley. Music bumped from the whole car like a pulse. It was a grotesque comment that remarked on both their bodies and implied the young man's desire to rape them. Ainsley and Mary did not look at the man and they did not look at each other. They gripped their backpack straps very tightly and looked straight ahead. The stopped car was clogging traffic and a truck behind it began to beep in impatience. The young men rolled up their window and sped away, and Ainsley and Mary continued their walk to their reading area, only Ainsley suggested that they cut away from the road, in between the trees. When they arrived at the town square park they sat down in exhaustion. Mary was tight-lipped and distracted while she read aloud. The noise from the distant traffic seemed particularly vehement. Ainsley, who was usually irritable if the reading conditions were not perfect, made no complaints or protestations. As Mary read from several psychology journals that posited theories about why one might have the desire to eat oneself Ainsley put her head in Mary's lap and listened. Almost all the books agreed that it was a sexual desire, an extension of the want to copulate with oneself, to put one's own flesh within one's body and have the power, through penetration, to bring oneself to orgasm.

"What if you have the desire to eat human flesh that isn't your own?" said Ainsley. "What if you want to eat someone else?"

Mary put the journal in her hand down on the bench. "Well, that seems like something else entirely," Mary said. "That seems more about possession, the desire to possess someone else so fully that you want to destroy them."

"But what if it's not about destruction," said Ainsley. "What if it's just about wanting to have sex?"

"Hold on," Mary said as she brought the book back to her face and started flipping the pages. "Maybe there is overlap? Between people who want to eat other people and people who want to eat themselves?"

"That would be very sad, to be that person," Ainsley said. "At least you can really eat someone else. At least that is a fantasy you could actually achieve. But eating yourself? You'll never really get that far."

"Well, that's the whole point of the ouroboros, isn't it? He did it," said Mary.

"We don't know he did it," said Ainsley.

"Well, the book implied it," said Mary. "The page following the illustrations was blank."

In one of the books Mary found an article on a man in Japan who wanted to eat both himself and other people. The Japanese man, she read, had, in fact, eaten someone else: a young French woman whom he had shot in the back of the head and put in his refrigerator. In the book there were several transcripts of him being interviewed by the psychiatrist who had written the article. Ainsley read the part of the transcripts that appeared to be the most interesting aloud:

Q: Is who you want to eat determined by their gender?

A: Yes. I have only ever wanted to eat women.

Q: When was the first time you knew you wanted to eat a woman?

A: When I knew I wanted to eat a little girl. I was a boy. I was in the first grade. Her name was Yui. She had straight long hair that her mother always put a purple bow in. When I forgot my pencil case one day, she let me borrow one of her pens. When she passed the pen to me, our hands touched, and I knew then that I wanted to eat her.

Q: Did you want to have sex with Yui?

A: I don't think I knew what sex was. I was in the first grade.

Q: But now, when you have the desire to eat a woman, do you want to have sex with her?

A: Yes.

Q: The French woman who you shot, did you want to have sex with her?

A: Yes.

Q: Before you shot her did you rape her?

A: No.

Q: After you shot her, did you rape her corpse?

A: No.

Q: Why not?

A: Because I was too excited about the prospect of eating her. I was too busy and too excited about carv-
ing off a part of her buttocks and putting it in my
mouth.

"I don't think this man really wants to eat himself,"
said Ainsley.

"Neither do I," said Mary. "He seems perfectly content
to eat someone else." Ainsley and Mary continued to discuss the psychology books they had read that morning
as the afternoon sun began to lower and hint at the coming evening. Other town residents, mostly young mothers,
or paid caregivers and the elderly, walked by their bench
throughout the day.

"They're looking at us," said Mary.

"Who?" said Ainsley. "The little old ladies?"

"Yes," said Mary. "Everybody is always looking at us."

"And we are always looking at other people," said Ainsley. "Most people are viewed at most points during the
day."

"But not everybody's viewing is the same," said Mary.
"These old park ladies aren't looking at us like the boys in
the car were looking at us. And I'm not looking at you like
they looked at me."

"Well, the car-boy way of looking at someone is violent, or at least implies violence," said Ainsley. "They could have just looked at us that way, without even saying anything, and their intent would have been the same."

"How do I look at you?" said Mary. "What does my gaze contain?"

"Questions," said Ainsley. "Which is the essential thing. When the car-boys looked at us, they didn't have any questions for us because they assumed we had nothing to offer them except our bodies, which required no questions because our bodies could already be seen."

At 1:00 p.m. Mary and Ainsley walked to a deli and ordered sandwiches. When they heard their numbers at the deli counter they thanked the man behind the counter, retrieved their white-butcher-paper-clad sandwiches, and walked back to the park. After they finished eating, Mary and Ainsley discussed the birds that flew above them, and decided that, in their next glut of books, they would see if they could get a book that would help them identify the birds that flew in the woods near their homes.

The rest of the summer, the last few weeks of it, went quickly. Mary and Ainsley had many things they wanted to do before they had to begin school. Mary had overheard a conversation about a swimming hole in the middle of the forest that they wanted to find and go to. Ainsley had several compulsory hikes that they must do. They both wanted to try and find a printing press that they could buy and use for art projects. By the time Labor Day approached they had found the swimming hole, but not the printing press. They entered high school that Tuesday, September 3, after everyone in the town had gotten that Labor Day Monday off. Mary and Ainsley's academic schedules were exactly the same, save Physical Education:

Mary	*Ainsley*
1° World History	1° World History
2° Honors Science	2° Honors Science
3° Spanish III	3° Spanish III
4° Algebra I	4° Algebra I
5° Study Hall	5° Physical Education
6° Honors English	6° Honors English

Mary would have soccer practice Monday through Thursday after school for an hour. She feared Ainsley would be angry that they wouldn't be able to walk home from school together. But, then again, Ainsley had wallowed and chosen PE.

"Why do you like playing soccer?" Ainsley asked Mary.

"Because it gives you a hint of the power your body possesses," said Mary. "I like feeling my calves tense and the smack of the ball against the inlay of my laces. There is a violence in it. It gives you a hint of the violence your body could do."

"Do you ever think about hurting anyone?" said Ainsley.

"All the time," said Mary. "Don't you?"

On the first day of class nothing much happened. They saw people they knew and people they didn't know. The school was big and ugly, a giant block of concrete that, Mary discovered, had been designed by an architect that was most famous for building prisons. There were grates on all the widows. Ainsley joked that somewhere on campus there must be a room that only contained padded walls.

In World History, Mary and Ainsley's teacher, Mr. Reignhart, made clear that his class would be a class about dead people, most often dead people from far-flung lands.

"What does he mean by 'far flung'?" Ainsley asked on their break between classes.

"I think he means civilizations that are dead enough that they couldn't possibly be a threat to us," said Mary.

"Oh, I see."

In Honors English, later that week, Mrs. Tulli gave the class a novel to read that was about a young woman whose father wanted her to find a suitor, but the young woman did not want a suitor, until the young woman realizes that one of the suitors pursuing her isn't that bad. Mary and Ainsley disliked the novel because they thought the young female protagonist was apathetic, and also, that she had a very flawed logic.

"The conversations in this book never make sense," said Ainsley. "The characters talk at each other like they're playing tennis."

"I've never played tennis," said Mary.

"Neither have I. But I know what it looks like, and I have certainly seen people talk like tennis looks," said Ainsley.

"But if a conversation was like tennis that implies that it would be continuous, that two people would push the same idea back and forth. And that's not what's happening in this book," said Mary. "In this book people are just chucking balls in the general direction of other characters, but nobody ever returns the same throw."

"You're right," said Ainsley. "I guess the conversations in this book are failed games of tennis."

"Would you ever play tennis with me?" asked Mary. "We could learn together. There are courts down by the community pool."

"I don't think so," said Ainsley. "The thought of having an additional appendage, such as a racket, seems highly difficult and unpleasant."

"I can understand that," said Mary. "There is so much one can athletically accomplish with the limbs that are already at our disposal. I think that is part of the reason why I like soccer."

"I don't like soccer," said Ainsley.

"I know."

That evening, when Mary went home, she was instructed to watch her little brother while her mother was in the kitchen. Mary's brother was very easy to watch because he was strapped into an apparatus, a kind of infant baby walker that had a built-in diaper strap that suspended him, standing. There was a tray that surrounded the reach of his arms and structural legs that possessed wheels so he could scoot himself across the hardwood floor of the living room by simply flailing his feet. The apparatus also had a structure above his head that looked like a cartoon rainbow. Toys hung from the rainbow by scrunchy fabric strings that Mary's little brother occasionally batted like a cat. He looked up at the toy sun that hung from the rainbow and swatted it, leaning forward as he did so and slightly pushing his apparatus in the direction of his swat. He was too small to really reach the toy sun, and ran his fun station on wheels into the edge of a carpet. He bunched his eyebrows and opened his toothless mouth as if he were going to scream. He sat there for a moment, silent, open-mouthed in his pre-tantrum. Mary looked at him in this state and thought it was one of the scariest things she had ever seen. The scream came forward and the brother dribbled spit. Mary's mother came out from the kitchen.

"Mary," she said. "What's wrong with your little brother?"

"He can't reach his toys," said Mary. "He's too small."

"Well then, can't you help him?" said Mary's mother, incensed, as she leaned into the brother's apparatus, pulled the hanging sun down to his outstretched hands, whereupon the brother promptly grabbed the toy and put it in his mouth.

"He thinks it's food," said Mary.

"No, he doesn't," said Mary's mother. "It's just his way of playing with it."

"By trying to eat it?" said Mary.

"Yes."

Mary and Ainsley met before school the next day to read together and discuss Mary's little brother. They sat on a picnic bench in the center quad and Ainsley read aloud from a psychology book that claimed, among other things, that opposites attract.

"I don't think opposites attract," said Mary. "I'm the

opposite of my brother but I'm not attracted to him. I am repulsed by him. I can talk, he can't. He needs my parents, while my parents need me. What could be more opposite and repulsive than that?"

"It does seem like a false claim," said Ainsley. "Or at least a conditional one. And you're right, true opposites don't attract, not even in the scientific sense. For instance, diamonds are not magnetically drawn to coal. But what I think this book is getting at is that if two people have a baseline in common, like with two people who are both able to speak and are both reasonably smart, then there is a likelihood that, within that baseline, you would be drawn to someone that is different from you."

"Everyone is different from you," said Mary. "If they weren't different from you then they'd be you and you can't be anyone else but yourself."

"But look," said Ainsley. "That is how Rose Red and Snow White work. Because they are opposites, their complementary nature is supposed to somehow be narratively more appealing. Their opposite nature is one of things that make them compelling."

"But they're not that different," said Mary. "The biggest difference between them is their hair color. They're both sisters, and they both turn into roses. And they both basically say the same thing the whole story, which is essentially just, 'O! Mister bear you're so scary and fun to play with! Why can you talk? Watch out for the goblin!' And then Red is dumb enough to marry the bear after he resumes his human prince form, but you kind of get the sense that White wants in on him, too. It is basically just like that book we read for Mrs. Tulli's class! Only more interesting, because in the end the girls turn into plants."

"Is it more interesting?" said Ainsley. "Snow White kind of sells out Rose Red in the end, by taking the more powerful suitor, the prince, for herself and, yes, they do turn into plants, but only roses, which is kind of a boring plant to choose to turn into."

"You're right," Mary said. "What if they turned into squash or heads of lettuce? I love squash. I think I would like to be a squash."

"Let's not call each other Red and White anymore," said Ainsley. "After reading that book for Mrs. Tulli's class, I don't find Rose Red and Snow White all that interesting, or imitation worthy. I am sure we can find something better to pretend we might be."

Later that day, Mary and Ainsley walked into Spanish III class together. Their teacher, Señora MacDonald, asked Ainsley to sit down and for Mary to come to the front of the class. Señora MacDonald wore a knee length leather skirt and a gray, sleeveless turtleneck. Her hair was a frizzy, carrot-colored mass and her lips were painted bright red. Señora MacDonald usually talked in Spanish at all times in the classroom, but now she spoke in English.

"Mary, please face your classmates," said Señora MacDonald. Mary stood in front of the classroom and faced her classmates. Mary took off her backpack and laid it on the floor. The whole class looked at Mary.

"Raise your hands above your head, Mary," said Señora MacDonald. Mary raised her hands above her head. Mary looked at Señora MacDonald and Señora MacDonald looked at Mary. Then, Señora MacDonald took her pointer finger and pointed it at the three inches of Mary's bare stomach, right above Mary's pant line.

"Midriff," said Señora MacDonald. "A clear violation of the dress code. These low-slung jeans and tight small shirts are not appropriate for a productive learning environment. Your job is to learn with your classmates, Mary, not distract them. You can put your hands down now. Please gather your things and go to the principal's office. Your absence during this class will show as unexcused."

Mary picked up her backpack and walked out the door to make her way to the principal's office. Ainsley sat red-faced and baffled, and thought for a moment she would stand up and go with Mary, make a march of it and walk out the door with her, but then Mary was gone and Señora MacDonald was talking again, this time in Spanish, and the moment seemed to have passed without anyone really taking note of it, so Ainsley resolved to stay in her seat and think, so that when she saw Mary again they could come up with a plan of action.

Inside the principal's office, Mary sat alone and waited for Mr. Flavin, the principal, with her palms clasped in her lap. While she waited, Mary went over the events in her head. She saw herself sitting in the chair across from Mr. Flavin's desk as if she were the principal. She saw herself standing in front of the Spanish class, arms overhead, the flesh of her belly exposed. She could feel Señora Mac-Donald's finger, her pointy painted nail touching the skin right above her hip bone, and the whole class' stare toward that finger, as if Señora MacDonald might actually push her finger right into Mary and skewer her, and then raise her up into the air impaled for all to see. Principal Flavin came in.

"Hello, Mary," said Mr. Flavin. "How are you today?"

"I am not well," said Mary.

"And why is that?" said Mr. Flavin.

"I believe you know why I am here, so I think you should be able to tell me," said Mary.

"Attitude!" said Mr. Flavin. "Just like your outfit! I can see this won't be the last time you'll be in trouble at this school."

"I don't understand why you think I have an attitude," said Mary.

"Let me explain something to you," said Mr. Flavin. "You are at a point in your life where you may not yet be aware that, to men, you are sexually attractive. Men want to have sex with you. And your outfit is encouraging men, your male classmates, to want to have sex with you, to think about having sex with you, when they should be thinking about school."

Once Principal Flavin finished speaking, he opened up his office door and Mary was allowed to walk to her next class, which was Algebra. Lucky for Mary and Ainsley, the whole Algebra period they were supposed to collaborate with a partner on a problem set, so they could talk to each other while they were working, and fill in each other on the details of their separate experiences during the last class period in which they had been apart.

"Do you think Principal Flavin wants to eat himself or other people?" asked Ainsley.

"Definitely other people," said Mary. "Mainly me."

"That would be terrible," said Ainsley. "His mouth looks like a catfish. I would not want my leg in his mouth."

"Neither would I," said Mary.

"What about Señora MacDonald?" said Ainsley. "Does she want to eat herself or other people?"

"I think she wants to eat herself, but only in the sense that she hates herself and is therefore looking for other people with which she can displace her own self-hatred. Or, maybe, she is just not very smart, and acts out some kind of perverse reflection of Principal Flavin's want to eat us? Like, she is controlled by him in some way, and therefore acts out his impulses for him?"

"Do you think it is really Principal Flavin who controls Señora MacDonald? Or is she controlled by something else?" said Ainsley.

"You're right," said Mary. "Who knows who controls Principal Flavin! He certainly isn't smart enough to control himself. He doesn't exist in a vacuum. I think my father might also be in Mr. Flavin's vacuum."

"I think my father might be, too."

Mary and Ainsley finished their math worksheets and turned them into Mr. Lockney. Then they exited the math classroom and went to lunch. They walked to center quad of the school where there was a small green. The four tall walls of the school rose around them, blocking much of the natural light. They put down their jackets on the lawn and sat facing each other with their legs crossed.

"I read a story once," said Ainsley. "That is kind of like what happened to you in Señora MacDonald's class, only, of course, much more explicit. Have you read the story of Daphne? That woman who got chased by Apollo and then turned into a tree?"

"Of course," said Mary. "We've read it together at my house, in my book of Greek myths."

"Right," said Ainsley. "Well this story is like the story of Daphne, only better, because you get more of the woman's thoughts and how exactly she escapes her pursuers. It's about a woman named Norea who lives in Egypt, who is being chased by a man who is a king, but some say he is the devil, and he has, with him, some of his other devil friends. The king and his friends run after Norea, and say, 'Norea we are going to rape you.' And then they come upon her and it looks like they have got her, like they are going to rape her, but then she wins. She turns her spirit into a tree and watches, from her tree-spirit eyes, as the kings rape what they think is her body, and she laughs at them because she's tricked them, because she's no longer in her body at all. Her real body, at that point, is the tree."

"It sounds like they killed her," said Mary. "And now the kings are just raping her dead body. I don't think she won. Dying doesn't count as winning."

Lunch ended and Mary and Ainsley parted ways for their respective Study Hall and Physical Education periods. After their last class, which was Mrs. Tulli's Honors English, Ainsley walked home and Mary went to soccer practice.

Waiting for practice to begin, Mary sat on a hot aluminum bench with the other girls in her soccer gear. Mary wore thin, plastic running shorts and a large T-shirt that had her father's college's name on it. She pulled on her shin guards, one by one, and then her big tube socks that had the pair of black stripes at the top, and then her cleats. The cleats smelled strongly of sweat and dirt because Mary had worn them while doing laps around the field over the summer. She had wanted to prepare for varsity tryouts and break in the shoes. Mary liked the feeling of running alone in her spiked footwear, and she felt that same feeling of euphoria now, at practice, as she ran around the goals at either end of the field and warmed up. After all the athletes were present, the team did many drills together, mostly where they had to run in lines in a relay and touch the grass with their hands to signify their completion of an interval. In between intervals they did drills with a ball. They bounced the balls on their knees, and controlled it, back and forth, between their feet, and took turns returning the ball, from a mid-flight throw with their head. Mary put her brow to the center of the ball three, four times, and then twenty. Her head got light and she could feel the dark at the edges of her eyes fuzz. Again, Mary said, again, and she headed the ball into an arc far away from her. Her dark brown curls bounced up and down and she pulled her arms back and plunged her chest forward, as she stiffened her neck and returned the throw. Mary could feel her blood hardening and her arms and legs growing stronger. This is what it feels like to turn into a tree, thought Mary. This is what it feels like to use your body hard enough that you leave it. I have to tell Ainsley about this feeling, thought Mary. Maybe then Ainsley would want to run.

Back at home, Ainsley read alone on her sofa. Ainsley had one sister who was six years older than she was, so the sister didn't live at home. Ainsley's mother watched television, which was Ainsley's mother's main occupation. Ainsley's father was a fireman, and thus was only home on and off, now being the off part, so the only people in the house were Ainsley and her mother. On the television was a reality TV show about girls from evangelical families who got raped and were made to keep the baby. On the screen was a gaggle of Ainsley's-age-looking women, who scooted around the TV set and yelled at their moms. Their bellies rounded slowly throughout the show, so that by the end of the episode Ainsley thought they looked like bloated dead bodies, their abdomens stretched so tight they looked plastic and as if, at any moment, they might explode. While watching the TV show, Ainsley had a vision of Señora MacDonald touching Mary's stomach and then Mary's stomach immediately expanding on finger impact, ballooning in a matter of seconds so that by the time Mary got to the classroom door she looked like she was just about to give birth. By the time the episode ended, it was late in the evening. All the lights in the house were off except for the blue light of the TV. Ainsley's mother was sleeping, her head tilted on the back of the couch, her mouth gaping, releasing a steady stream of hot, gaseous air. Their dog, a white toy poodle named Roofus, was licking Ainsley's mother's arm raw. A soft pink patch of skin appeared on her forearm where Roofus had licked. Ainsley turned off the television and put a blanket over her mother and Roofus and then went to sleep.

During the night Ainsley dreamed of summer camp. She saw her eight-year-old self clad in her camp uniform. The camp was all girls. All the girls made lanyards and learned about owls and the contents of owl pellets. Ainsley saw herself picking apart owl dung with a pair of tweezers, pulling out snake bones and rat hair and what looked like a venomous fang. Then she saw herself on a hike with her cabin unit. They were traversing the side of a mountain, going straight from the bottom up to the peak. Their unit leader was a college-aged woman. She had a tanned leather face and crooked teeth and black hair underneath both of her arms. She led a group of around thirty campers, Ainsley among them. As they climbed up the mountain they periodically crossed a winding road made for cars. When they came to the asphalt they would have to look left, checking for oncoming vehicles, and then right. The first couple times they crossed the road there were no cars in either direction. Then, they came to a crossing, and the unit leader spotted a car. The unit leader turned to them, her herd of little girls, their little red bandanas sticking to their wet little necks. She halted them with her hand and said, "Be a tree!" as she raised her arms in demonstration, putting her arms over her head bent at awkward angles as if her arms were branches about to spring leaves. She rooted her feet to the ground and stood perfectly still. And then there was silence. The mass of little girls faced her like well-trained warriors, their arms raised overhead in imitation. There was not even a hush. And then, the car was upon them, a red truck speeding fast around the turn where the campers were foresting, dangerously pummeling up the mountain to wherever the driver was going, possibly his home. "Good work, campers," said the unit leader. "When you a see a car coming, what's the safest thing to do?" The unit leader put her hand to her ear to mime her want for the girls' collective response, "Get off the road and be a tree!" The campers all yelled in unison, their little-girl voices echoing in the mountains, their little-girl chatter and giggles bubbling back up into being, their plant forms leaving, their girl forms returning to their little girl heads. Eight-year-old Ainsley stomped her hiking boots in the dirt path of the mountain and looked down below at the lake far beneath them. She was looking forward to reaching the peak of the hike. She wanted so badly to see how small the lake could get, if one could get high enough up where the lake actually turned into nothing. It was a very big lake, so she didn't think it could ever, actually, turn into nothing. But she thought it was possible, even probable, that, viewed from that high up, what the lake looked like would change.

The next day at school Ainsley told Mary the story of her childhood summer camp dream remembering.

"Did you actually go to summer camp?" asked Mary.

"Yes," said Ainsley. "The dream was more night-time memory than fantasy, actually."

"It sounds like it was fun," said Mary. "I wish we had been friends then so I could have asked my mom if I could go."

"It was fun," said Ainsley. "In any case, I think I have come up with a plan of action."

"Really?" said Mary. "I think I have a possible plan of action, too."

"Well," said Ainsley. "I think this all has to do with eating. Right now we are being actively eaten but we aren't eating anyone."

"Exactly!" said Mary. "It's about consumption. We have to consume so we're not consumed."

"Now, I know we could look at this all in a larger context," said Mary. "But I kind of get the feeling that the idea of a larger context is a dangerous notion that denies the injustice of what has occurred. If we focus on justice at the local level, I think it will imply justice at the larger level, and that is, I think, what we need."

"But it is a web," said Ainsley. "A sticky film certainly connects everything. Especially in this situation, in which, I fear, everyone who lives within a thirty-five mile radius of our school is implied."

"OK," said Mary. "I think you're right, but we can't kill all of them."

"We can if we can kill a symbol of them," said Ainsley.

"What about my little brother?" said Mary. "We could kill him."

"He is disgusting," said Ainsley. "But is he implied?"

"Have you seen his small little dick?" said Mary.

"No," said Ainsley.

"All he wants to do is consume," said Mary. "Sure, he can't yet yell at us from a car, and he doesn't yet have the dexterity to molest, but the intent is there. If he knew what sex was, that's what he'd want from us. It's like the Japanese cannibal. He knew he wanted to eat someone before he knew what anything else was. You can see it in my brother's eyes. He's the same way. And he's a symbol that extends to all of them: the men in the car, Señora Mac-

Donald, and Mr. Flavin. They'll be very sorry when my brother is dead because they see something of themselves in him. It's the most powerful way to kill all of them."

"I guess you're right," said Ainsley.

"I was thinking it would be best to boil him," said Mary. "Like they do with lobsters on TV."

"Do you think his skin will fall off?" said Ainsley.

"Probably," said Mary. "Maybe then we can see the meat of him, that man meat he's made of. We'll take pictures of his meat and send a note to Mr. Flavin with the picture and write 'Who's eating who? Beware! We'd like to eat you.'"

"Will Mr. Flavin get it, though?" said Ainsley.

"Who cares," said Mary. "I don't think it's our job to make his brain work better. He'll be scared, which is the important thing. Maybe it's even better if he doesn't put two and two together."

"You're right," said Ainsley. "That is always the scariest part of any movie—when things are unclear and hard to understand."

"Really though," said Mary. "I think we have to kill someone. What else is there for us to do?"

"We could keep watching," said Ainsley. "Until we know exactly how everything works. Like our ouroboros we could try being 'active and passive at the same time.'"

"That sounds really painful and boring," said Mary. "And what if they eat us first? It is eat or be eaten, Ainsley!"

"Be patient," said Ainsley. "We'll eat them. We just need to figure out the best way how."

In Honors Science, that day, Mary and Ainsley were

tasked with doing a partnered research project on their choice of phylum. They sat at their lab station, sink, Bunsen burner, and a fat science textbook between them.

"I want to research parthenogenetic snakes," said Mary.

"Like the ouroboros?" said Ainsley.

"It was unclear to me if the ouroboros is capable of a virgin birth," said Mary.

"Sure, it is," said Ainsley. "We know it 'weds and impregnates itself, that it is both man and woman, begetting and conceiving at the same time.'"

"That sounds more like a hermaphrodite," said Mary. "Like it still needs something else, another snake to mate with."

"No, it doesn't," said Ainsley. "It does the begetting AND the conceiving. It's a one-woman job through and through."

"I guess you're right," said Mary.

"But which snake species are parthenogenetic?" said Ainsley. "I thought it was something female snakes only did, rarely, when kept in captivity, like a last-ditch biological feat to keep their species alive because they are alone in a box and think the world has ended and there are no more males anywhere with which to mate."

"Didn't you watch that TV episode with me?" said Mary. "The one where they revealed that that hypothesis was a fallacy, and that snakes and other reptiles have been reproducing asexually in the wild for ages, and that it is possible that some species could become all female? Why would they need males, after all, if they could do the whole job themselves?"

"I must have fallen asleep," said Ainsley, looking disappointed.

"What a bunch of numbskulls," said Mary. "Assuming something could only be done in captivity, when their only test subjects were in captivity."

"Are we in captivity?" said Ainsley.

"Of sorts," said Mary, as she smiled.

"You know who else, besides certain types of snakes, are capable of parthenogenesis?" said Ainsley, slyly, her eyebrows raised in giddy anticipation.

"Who?" said Mary.

"Plants," said Ainsley, as she dug her hand deep into their science textbook, flipped the page and read aloud.

HUNKER DOWN
\\\\\\\\\\\\\\\\\\\

BY THE TIME MY DAUGHTER came of age, the economy was so bad that it was cheaper to hire someone to hold her breasts up than it was to buy her a bra. We put an ad on Craigslist and decided Mark was the best fit for the position. We set him up in our backyard with some water and a shack. He would get up every morning at the crack of dawn and stand outside her room and wait for her to rise. When she left the house, Mark hunched over and slid his hands underneath her shirt, cupping my daughter's small breasts gently. He scurried behind her, head tucked down, providing the best support that any parent could ask for. He was an older gentleman who, if the times were different, would have been just over the age bracket of a young professional. I believe he sent the money he made working for us to his parents.

Mark's solitary flaw as a breast holder was that he was only useful short-term. The hunching and cupping gave him severe back problems that eventually prevented him from working all of the necessary hours. In our family finance meeting, we reasoned that the lifespan of a breast holder was similar to that of a laptop—after four years their efficiency slowed until inevitably, they crashed, and were no longer of use. Mark crashed the day his riddled arthritic hands formed tight fists that couldn't hold anything, let alone my daughter's precious breasts. We replaced Mark with Evan, but kept Mark on for a short time so he could train our new hire. The two of them, Evan and Mark, could be seen before dawn in dutiful practice—hunching over in the dark, cupping air and pacing the length of our lawn. They walked in long lines and then stood still for fifteen minute intervals, testing their conversation support stance, and would finally end their predawn training session with a brief cupping jog meant to simulate my daughter's commendable routine of exercise. After Evan's training was complete, we brought Mark back to the place from which we had picked him up—a small hillock several miles outside of town. As we drove to drop off Mark at the hillock, my daughter's new breast holder, Evan, sat in the back seat, reaching around the sides of the front seat to put his hands under my daughter's shirt and support her. When we arrived at the hillock I had to put the car in park to let Mark out. His hands had become so

clenched that even pulling open the door handle was beyond his capabilities. Once outside the car, Mark dropped
to all fours. As I climbed back into the driver's seat, Evan
voiced a heartfelt request to briefly lapse in his responsibilities. I gave him permission to do so, and he pulled his
left hand out from under my daughter's shirt and waved to
Mark as we drove away.

DECOR
\\\\\\\\\\\\\\\\\\\\

THERE WAS A PERIOD of my life in which my primary source of income came from being a piece of furniture. I worked for a business that sold sofas that cost over six times what I was paid in a year. The showroom was on the twenty-fourth floor of a beautiful modern building in the Flatiron District of Manhattan. There was no storefront. It was a word-of-mouth business. If you were rich enough, you knew about it. The clients were Saudi princes looking to spend $80,000 on a dining table; creative directors of high-end fashion companies looking to overhaul their runway seating, buy a million or two million dollars' worth of luxury benches; hobbled old Upper East Side women redesigning their Hampton homes, budgets of five million and up just to acquire objects, things to fill the spaces they already owned.

A big floor-to-ceiling stainless-steel door opened from the hallway into the show space. Inside the show space were several interior configurations—dining rooms and living rooms and bedrooms set up on circles of carpet— living quarters that in real life would have been divided but here, in the showroom, were smashed up against each other without any walls. And on the other side of the imaginary rooms, just below the big windows, was me, at a long grand desk, in a pencil skirt. I was a pretty, young girl who brought the clients almonds and glasses of wine. I also opened the mail, coordinated the shipping, and did a great deal of filing. But I understood that my primary purpose was my presence. I added to the atmosphere, my employers told me. I added something to the experience of the showroom that my colleagues, all gay men over fifty, couldn't provide.

My colleagues loved having me in the showroom. They said I was beautiful. They said I dressed fashionably. They said my short hair was avant-garde. It is true that I do like beautiful clothing. I feel most at home in prints that are loud. I like objects that startle me when I look at them.

I didn't mind being looked at as much at the beginning. One man, during the early months of my employment, came into the showroom and asked to take photographs of me sitting on the furniture. He said he wanted a human element in the pictures, something that would help him remember the proportions and size. I sat on the chaise lounge and curled my high-heeled feet up under me. I put my hands behind my head and tried to look deadpan. Perfect, said the man. He never bought anything. I would have known if he had because I filed all the orders, knew exactly who bought what and how much money was coming in.

When I opened the mail, there were often requests for samples, architects or interior designers wanting to see a swatch of the wood grain or the fabric or the leather used on a particular design. In the morning I made a stack of the letters that requested swatches. In the afternoon I went into the back room, a dingy windowless closet, and found what each person wanted and then sent them the sample. Sometimes people also requested catalogs or lookbooks, big-format photographs of the furniture placed in front of the ocean on a sandy beach, a ridiculous situation akin to a woman in a ball gown on an elephant, which, in fashion magazines, you do often see.

I had been working in the showroom for six months when I got the letter. I didn't immediately know if I was going to show it to my boss. It was a nondescript, cheap business envelope. The showroom address and the return address were written by hand. The return address said *State Correctional Institution—Frackville, Pennsylvania*. Inside the envelope was a piece of paper that appeared to be a photocopy of a letter that had been typed on a typewriter. The paper had the lines and dark spots that come with a sloppily executed photocopy. Stapled to the letter was a note the size of Post-it that said I, the recipient, should be aware that all prison correspondence is read and monitored. The letter itself was short, but alarmingly articulate. The contents were very strange and upsetting. The worst part about it was how overly formal the whole thing was. It said:

Dear Sir or Madam,

You do not know me, and so I understand that it will therefore be difficult to persuade you to perform the task which I request. My name is Malcolm Danvers and I am currently incarcerated. I spend most of my time in solitary confinement. Alone in this black box I have little joy. Therefore, I have taken to imagining for myself a new home. A new structure that I could build upon my release, a modern structure that I could build in the woods and live in. After being here, in this cell for so long, I no longer believe I am fit for human company. So the only thing I can do, the only thing that keeps me alive, is to imagine a beautiful life for myself, alone, outside this prison. An architecturally stunning feat that brings in lots of light. I have read many books, while imprisoned, on drafting architectural plans and have thus, in the last two years, already established an achievable blueprint. I am now at the stage where interiors must be considered. I have been made to understand that your pieces are some of the best, some of the most elegant in the business, and that any one of your designs can be custom-made. This aspect of your product is of great interest to me because it allows me an even greater breadth of imagination. Therefore, I have a request of you. If you can, would you be kind enough to send me several catalogs of your best-selling pieces, and also some samples, so that I might imagine more vividly the furniture in my woods-circled home? Any leather or fabric swatches would be of great value to me. Unfortunately, due to the constraints of my situation, I cannot accept fabric or leather samples bigger than 1" × 1" because of their potential to be used as a weapon. Similarly, I am unable to accept any wood or metal samples because of their violent potential. Thank you, dear sir or madam, for considering this request. I realize that in your office and your life you are, no doubt, a person of extreme importance and already under a great deal of demands as it stands. Any time you could take to send me some samples and catalogs would be greatly appreciated. Perhaps it will give you joy, at least, to picture some of your beautiful furniture in the home of my imagination, looking elegant and stunning in the morning light.

In gratitude,
Mr. Malcolm Danvers

I remember putting the letter down in something of a panic. I feared someone was watching me, as I often feared during the workday. My colleagues were very nosy and frequently asked me what I was doing, what I was working on, which task I had at hand. I knew that if I showed the letter to my boss he would be disgusted and make me throw it away. I may have been wrong about this, but I could sense they would not think the letter was of interest. They would probably be primarily concerned with trying to figure out how this man in jail had gotten our name. I couldn't decide what to do so I put the letter in my purse and brought it home with me that evening.

I knew I could probably find out online what this man had done to land himself in prison. But then I thought that this was, maybe, something I didn't want to know. Perhaps if I were a better person, I would have looked it up immediately. But I had been made aware, during this time in my life, that I was not as good a person as many of my friends were, specifically when it came to contemplating the death penalty, which it seemed Mr. Malcolm Danvers was not at risk for. But maybe he had narrowly escaped. What I mean is, in the social circles I associated with, there were a lot of young liberal-minded people, people who were sexual extremists and in polyamorous relationships and who also were deeply invested in prison reform, despite never having had contact with a prisoner in their entire lives. It was not acceptable to believe in the death penalty, in my social group, and I had been alarmed, at recent evening gatherings and gallery openings, that when the subject of the death penalty came up, I found myself sympathetic. People were bad and they did terrible things. What use was it keeping these bad people alive?

This wasn't an opinion I voiced, ever. It would have been socially unacceptable to say out loud that perhaps some people are meant to die. Also, I usually didn't say much, so it would have been out of character for me to blurt it out. It just seemed to me, as I had experienced in my own life, that true evil did exist and that when it did infect someone it was incurable, and that those people should be killed. I thought of a man from my hometown who broke into fifteen houses and raped fourteen women. This man, I thought, should be dead. I could not conceive of a reason why this man should be alive. What was more, because he had not killed any of the women he would be, after seventeen years, released back out into the world. When I was sixteen and these crimes were being committed, I thought about killing him.

But what I mean to say is that I knew that because of my belief in true evil I could not look up the crimes of Mr. Malcolm Danvers. If I did and it was bad enough, then I would not be able to think about him or contemplate any further his imagined home. I wanted to give Danvers the samples because I wanted the feeling of privilege I'd get from giving another human an object of his wanting. If I looked him up I might not be able to send him any fabric swatches or obtain any possible joy from giving him these things because there would be a possibility that I would want to kill him. If I were another person—a bigger, smarter, more intellectual person—perhaps I could have immediately stomached whatever he had done, but I knew I wasn't, and I still wanted, for a little while longer, to think of him as human, so I did not look him up and the next morning went into the showroom and sent him the samples and the catalogs straightaway.

After I sent him the package, I felt good immediately. I sat at my big beautiful desk under those grand twenty-fourth-story windows and basked in the sun. I had signed my return letter with my real name. I told him, Here you are, Mr. Malcolm Danvers, may your home be every bit as beautiful as you have imagined. Yours, Ursula G.

I remember very vividly the rest of that day. Three clients came in and I was exceptionally friendly and sat with them while they drank their wine and talked about the problems they were having training a new dog. I remember specifically Mrs. Sheffield, one of our better Upper East Side old women clients, saying that her poodle refused to pee anywhere but everywhere. I thought of the $100,000 Turkish rug we had sold her the month previous. I hoped that the dog had made a pee river on that rug and really let its bowels run free.

Perhaps getting the letter was a turning point for my time in the showroom. When the letter came, I had been there about six months, long enough for the novelty to wear off and for me to figure out exactly what, regarding the purpose of my presence, was going on. I was so grateful for the job when I got it. Before I worked at the showroom I worked for a Chelsea boutique folding $300 T-shirts and steaming silk dresses in a windowless basement after the store closed. My usual work hours had been from 8:00 p.m. to 2:00 a.m. I listened to my iPod while I folded and felt very claustrophobic and very depressed. Perhaps a smarter person would have found some way to multitask, some way to use that time more effectively, but all I could feel while I was folding was that I was suffocating in a dark room, which I very well might have been, so when I got the job at the showroom through a friend of a friend, I felt I had landed in a palace on the moon. I mean, there were many things about the showroom that were both moonlike and palacelike. The world that lived in the showroom was completely detached from the world I knew. It was a place where the wealthiest people on the planet could act as if the way they lived their lives was acceptable. And even the furniture, the made-up room configurations, seemed to exist in a space devoid of gravity—free-floating rooms attached to nothing that simply implied life or the way someone might live a life in a home that did not actually contain humans or anything that was alive. And the palatial quality of it all, of being in a space where everything was the finest, made by the finest designers with the finest materials by the finest Italian craftsmen, implied that this was the best man could do: here in the showroom we were at the pinnacle of human creation. The best things money could buy, myself among them. It felt good to be around such fine things.

So at first, as I said, I didn't mind being viewed and being part of the furniture, because it felt good to be considered suitable company for such beautiful objects, and I had, before coming to the showroom, been a ghost that lived only at night, in the basement of a boutique, folding things and wishing I were smart enough to imagine a way out.

A month passed before I got another letter from Mr. Malcolm Danvers. It came the same way, in the mail, typed on a typewriter but photocopied, only this time he also sent architectural plans and it was addressed to me, Ms. Ursula G., which obviously caused me a great deal of alarm. I worried someone else in the showroom had seen it. It said:

My Dear Ursula,

Words cannot express the gratitude I feel for you. The leather you sent me is perfect for the low modern sofa I've put in the living room, and I am using several of the fabric samples you provided on lounge chairs throughout the house. Specifically, that dark gray linen has been upholstered on a design I saw and tore out from a feature on Italian innovators in Architectural Digest. *As you can see from the attached blueprints, your signature low sofa is perfect for the space in the left corner of the living room. I cut out the photo of it from the catalog you mailed and have taped it on the wall right next to my bed, where I lay my head to rest at night, along with your fabric and leather samples, so that I see my house, and your beautiful furniture in it, right before I sleep. I can think of no way to repay you for the gorgeous furniture you have gifted my imagination. I only wish I could have you over to my home, in its finished state, to serve you tea and to be able to show you all the magnificent work I have done and with which you have so graciously aided. Perhaps I can imagine this exchange, even if it never will, in the world outside this black box, transpire? If you feel generous, and would like to come to tea, send me a photo of yourself, and I will imagine you inside my beautiful home sitting on some of your stunningly designed modern furniture, me serving you tea and maybe some fresh biscuits.*

Yours,
Mr. Malcolm Danvers

I believe I shook slightly as I looked at the architectural plans. I remember sweating a great deal. They were well drawn and very professional looking. I wouldn't have been able to tell they were done by an amateur, let alone by a prisoner. I saw our signature low sofa drawn in miniature in the living room, just as Danvers had noted, and I saw the dark gray linen lounge chair, drawn in acute detail, smaller than the head of an eraser, in a room marked STUDY, and several more notations that communicated other furniture that he must have found from other companies, convinced other people to send to him and to correspond with him. It made me feel a little better that I was not the only one helping him build this home of his imagination. But it also made me feel a little jealous. I had been taken by the idea that I was somehow a unique savior to him, that I alone was helping his dream live on. I mean, I had been taken by the nature of it from the beginning, the idea that someone who lived only in darkness could build for themselves another world to inhabit. It was romantic. And deeply human, this notion that someone would want to construct for themselves a home they could never have, a home they could only ever go to when they closed their eyes.

But Danvers seemed to be somewhat convinced that he might actually get out and that he might actually be able to make his plans a reality. So then I had to reckon with the idea that I could, possibly, be helping him build a hideout, someplace for him to go after he had been released. I was very upset, thinking that this man, a man who probably did do something that would make me wish him dead, wanted to have me over in a room in his imagination.

It was a busy day in the showroom and I had lots to do, so I put the letter and the architectural plans in my purse and got to filing. By the time I got off work, my nerves had calmed. That evening I went to a dinner party, a long-standing arrangement where I would meet three friends of mine, some of the friends from the gallery openings, at one of their apartments for a meal. I picked up a bottle of wine on my way. I didn't plan to say anything about Mr. Malcolm Danvers at dinner, but then I had three glasses of wine and it just kind of came out. Marie, the woman whose apartment I was in, asked me about my day at work, and I told her about the letter. Everyone else became very interested in what I was saying and wanted to listen in. Suzanne, Marie's closest friend, said she felt very bad for Danvers, what a horror our prison system was, simple barbarism. Marie asked if I had been able to find out what Mr. Malcolm Danvers had done. No, I admitted, I didn't want to know. You should look it up, said Marie, especially now that he has asked for your picture, don't you want to know what he has done so you can better gauge how to respond to his letter? None of these people could sense my hidden belief that some people deserved to die. They wanted to look Danvers up, right then and there, but I begged them not to. No, I said, please, I don't want to know.

In an attempt to distract them, to change the subject, I pulled out the architectural plans that Danvers had attached to his second letter. I showed them the signature

low sofa and the linen lounge chair and they oohed and aa-
hed. Stephen, Marie's boyfriend, who I had forgotten was
an architect, examined the plans very intently and said,
It's a glass house, these demarcations here on the side mean
the paneling should be glass instead of wood. That makes
sense to me, I told him. Danvers said he wanted to let all
the light in, I guess that's what I would want too if I were
trapped indoors. Everyone at the dinner thought this was
very beautiful, Mr. Malcolm Danvers's desire for beauty
and a home and light, and Suzanne said it was everything
she could do to keep from crying.

This angered me slightly. Nobody seemed concerned
that Danvers wanted a picture of me to put in his home,
that he wanted me to be there with him in the woods in
his glass house having a cup of tea. It occurred to me then
that in this group of friends, I might also be a piece of
furniture. Was I something they kept around because I
looked avant-garde? I suppose it was at this dinner party
that I first reflected on whether or not the kind of life I
was living was lonely. And if the type of life I was living
was lonely, what other lives were there? Why did I feel so
wholly inanimate? Why did I feel so completely that I was
stuffed in a tightly sealed box? I had made great efforts to
relieve myself of this boxness. I dressed adventurously. I
consumed art. I read widely. So why did the idea that I,
like Mr. Malcolm Danvers, might too need an imaginary
house to build seem so true?

Stephen got up from the table and went into a bedroom
and returned with a laptop. I'm too curious, he said, I'm
too interested in the immaculate tragedy of it. I am going

to look our incarcerated architect up. *Our* incarcerated architect? I thought. How dare you. I was the one who sent him the samples, I was the one who wrote him a letter, I'm the one who's now being forced to have tea in the house of his mind. He's mine.

Please don't, I said to him, really, I mean it. Marie looked at me playfully and said, Come on now, Ursula, let us have our bit of fun. Everyone huddled around Stephen as he typed in the information. I tried to keep it together as the round circle that signaled the computer search thinking spun around and chased its own tail. Damn, said Stephen, let me restart it.

In this lull I tried, in my drunken state, to get ahold of how I was feeling. My hands were gripped to my knees and no one was looking at me, no one was paying me any heed at all. The conversation had taken off without me and had no need of me. All I had at that moment at that wretched dinner party was my imagined Danvers and what he could, depending on what he had done, mean to me. Danvers's desire to build something of beauty had touched me. I had an image of him in my head, some older man, gently feeling the fabric I sent him, that I couldn't shake off. I was scared of myself, scared to see how I felt about anyone who had done something bad enough to get stuck in a black box, and scared to admit that, in all likelihood, he deserved it. He probably deserved to be dead. I tried to be optimistic. Maybe he had been wrongly accused. Maybe he killed someone, but that someone was a very bad person. He spoke so articulately and had shown me, generously, the depths of his imagination. What types of crimes require imagination? To calm myself I made a list in my head of the worst possible things Danvers could have done: raped a child, raped many children, raped many women, killed many people, raped and killed a young woman who looked like me. Stephen came back to the table and typed MALCOLM DANVERS CRIMINAL RECORD into the search engine and it came up immediately—child pornography ring bust, biggest in Pennsylvania history, creator and distributor Malcolm Danvers put behind bars for only fifteen years because they couldn't find any evidence that he killed them, although eleven of the girls used in his videos (ages eight—thirteen) still couldn't be found.

Mr. Malcolm Danvers, I thought, Mr. Malcolm Danvers you are a murderer and a rapist.

Jesus, said Stephen.

Are you happy? I asked them. Should we go protest for his release?

Calm down, said Marie.

Why don't you write him? I said to her. Why don't you tell him how sorry you are that he has to be in there all alone? Maybe you should go visit him? Pennsylvania isn't that far away, maybe we should all go there together and express our deep regret at the injustice of his internment and the inhumanity of solitary confinement? Maybe we should send his architectural plans to the homes of the girls he raped, to the families of the victims, so they can sleep well knowing that Danvers has a very nice, luxurious home?

Drunk and infuriated, crazed by the fact that I felt I had had my reality violated by this information I so did not want to know, I goaded Stephen to keep going, keep searching, keep digging for more information that would make me want Malcolm Danvers dead. Stephen didn't respond, and only looked at me silently with his brows furrowed, so I took his computer from him. Why don't we search for images? I yelled at him.

Hundreds of photos came up, but they weren't photos of Danvers after his arrest. Rather, they were pictures of him well dressed, beaming, clearly communicating him as a real estate agent for multimillion-dollar homes. One of the photos was surrounded by text in a way that showed it was excerpted from a magazine. Under a photo of Danvers sitting in a living room was the caption PHILADEL-PHIA REAL ESTATE AGENT MR. MALCOLM DANVERS IN HIS OWN HOME. My god, I thought as I looked at the photo, Mr. Malcolm Danvers, you might use children like furniture, but you have very nice decor. In the photo you could see a great deal of his interiors. There was an Eames chair and a large fine kilim woven rug and expensive mahogany wood floors. On a modern, glass coffee table sat a design book. I could even make out the title—*The French Inspired Home*. I thought back to the man who had taken photos of me in the showroom, the man who had wanted a human element in the photographs of the furniture. What was the human element in this photograph of Mr. Malcolm Danvers? Where was the humanity here?

I looked at Stephen and Marie and Suzanne. What do you think of his taste? I yelled at them. Do you think he chose a nice color for the leather on his Eames chair?

Stephen said he was sorry for looking everything up,

that he didn't know how upset it would make me, a terrible half limp of an apology that somehow placed the blame back on my shoulders, back on the fact that I was the one screaming and ruining all that they had enjoyed about their evening, as if without me they'd have had Danvers all to themselves to contemplate and enjoy.

I could feel it then that I had threatened them, threatened their nice cutlery and their beautiful handmade dishware and their abstract, geometric prints that hung on hooks above their sink.

I kept yelling at them, asking them loudly where they got their gorgeous outfits. I complimented everything in the apartment at a deafening volume. I walked into the bathroom and said, These tiles are the most beautiful white. They're perfectly minimalist, I yelled. They do a perfect job at not being noticed.

I could hear Marie and Suzanne at the edges of my awareness, whispering in the living room about what to do with me. Stephen came into the bathroom, where I was rubbing their towels against my hand, and offered me more words that lacked an actual apology, and then asked if I would like it if he called me a cab home.

No, I said. I'll walk out of this apartment. And I did. And then I walked alone under the light-swollen city sky the many miles it took to get to the room where I slept.

I WOKE UP EARLY the next day, at 4:00 a.m., feeling ill and empty. I climbed out of my bedroom window and onto my fire escape, where I sat and watched the sun creep over the adjacent brownstones and thought of what I would send Danvers in return. I could just send him a printout of his conviction summary. A simple message—I know what you've done. But what would that do? It would perhaps incite shame, or just disappointment at being found out. Maybe that was how all his prison correspondence went— generosity and then shame. I do think shame is a useful weapon, but it relies so heavily on the person's own self-hatred, and maybe Danvers didn't really hate himself at all. I wanted to make Danvers feel the worst thing I had ever felt. Make no mistake, if I could have, I would have killed him. People that evil aren't ever cured. It's crazy to me that someone could look at that photograph of Danvers grinning in his luxury home, know what he had done, see his eyes, and ever think that this was a man who should go on living.

I knew that if the gallery opening friends ever heard me talk like this they'd mumble about cruel and unusual punishment and forgiveness for even the worst crimes, some rhetoric that, while true and intelligent, would only prove to me that they had never experienced violence in their own lives.

And then it came to me. I knew what I had to do. I needed to send Danvers something that would make him feel less living.

Earlier that year I had seen an exhibit at the Metropolitan Museum of Art on the furniture of Louis XIV, a fat man who was obsessed with the svelteness of his own legs, who thought he was king of the sun, and who also very much liked furniture that imitated beastliness. His chairs had the legs of deer, his sofas were made from pelts of lions, the hooves of horses were used all over his house to hold up pots or gold urns. It disturbed me when I saw the exhibit, those lion paws holding up Louis's favorite seat. This was perhaps the best way, or the only way, I knew to degrade Mr. Malcolm Danvers.

As soon as the image came to me I felt much more at ease. I could sketch Danvers into a piece of furniture in the style of Louis XIV, make his hairy arms the front legs of a sofa and his toed feet the back. I'd upholster it in a combination of Danvers's skin and that dark linen from his coveted lounge chair.

I went inside and got my notebook. I made an incredibly detailed sketch, and drew Danvers's head mounted at the center of the back of this baroque sofa, right where Louis XIV always put the sun. I drew the back of the sofa scalloped. I drew the arms as intricately carved wood that bent with the curve of the seat.

At 6:00 a.m. I got dressed and went in to the showroom, several hours before everyone else arrived. I made color photocopies of my drawing. I even shrank down my Danvers sofa to a small enough size that I could fit it on his blueprint. I put it right in front of his fireplace, where his skin would singe. Then, using the copier, I zoomed in on the beige sketch of the skin that I had drawn and printed off several color copies. After they were printed I taped them together to make a large 2' × 2' swatch of Danvers's skin. I put my drawing of the Danvers sofa and his blueprint with my added product placement in an envelope that was 8" × 11". I then wrapped the envelope in my Danvers skin paper and addressed it and walked down the stairs and placed the envelope in the public USPS mailbox on Sixth and Fourteenth.

As I slid the envelope into the blue metal slot I imagined Danvers opening the letter slowly, the seal of my skin package already broken by prison wardens who probably hated Danvers as much as I did, prison wardens who would relish letting my hate mail slide by. I imagined Danvers poring over my plans, poring over my drawings, with a confusion that slowly morphed into fear when he realized that I fully intended to cut off his ankles, if I had the chance, to make them into the footrests for kitchen stools, his knuckles the decorative knobs on the bars where I would rest my feet, and that in this house of my imagination he'd be murdered, murdered in the type of way that the murdered person's defining characteristic becomes how they were made into the dead.

I thought of him in prison, dismembered and inanimate, and imagined him finally realizing that he was no longer a man, just a thing in a house that would never be built, and would never be visited—a house that would disintegrate when I died because the mind that held it would melt into liquid and rot as soon as oxygen seeped inside.

This imagining hovered there for a moment, in the air above my head on Sixth and Fourteenth, and it felt good to look at it, and claim it, and acknowledge at least within myself that it was a creation that was mine. As I walked away from the mailbox I could feel the imagining following me. It hovered above my head. When I returned to the showroom to start my day at work, I could still feel it upon me, clamping the crown of my head as jewel settings prong a stone, and so when my boss called a meeting in the afternoon, I had trouble understanding what it was, exactly, he was saying, though I could hear his words perfectly fine.

There was going to be an overhaul of the company image, he said. We had previously carried many fine wood products, beautiful mahogany tables and chairs, beechwood outdoor chaises, but this was going to change. Within the interior design world, open-grain wood furniture is referred to as a living aesthetic, as in, the product's visual presence reveals that it did, in fact, come from a living thing. The living aesthetic is associated with rustic interiors, specifically those made by Scandinavian designers, who pioneered the realm of reclaimed wood. My boss said that this trend had become so popular that it had escaped the world of high design and invaded the mainstream. One could now buy wood-grain wallpaper at Target or pick up an open-grain table from Crate and Barrel on the cheap. This market, we were told in our meeting, was no longer something we were interested in serving. From here on out there would be no more open-grain wood, no more raw leather available from our showroom. The showroom would now exclusively embody a non-living aesthetic. New lookbooks were already being made. There was going to be a lot more chrome, and a lot more white leather, and many more big glass boxes, which, my boss told us, were chairs.

The open-grain sample showroom furniture got lacquered over. I coordinated shipping the pieces to the workshop and they came back shiny, white, and gray.

I could see myself in the reflection of their top coats. Chrome and lacquer scratch easily, my boss told me, so be careful of your rings. I wondered if the aesthetic change in the showroom demanded I now dress differently. Was there a way I could make myself look less living? Was my shaggy cropped hair too rustic, too suggestive that I too had once come from a living thing? How could I make myself more severe? I imagined my insides dissolving from their wet earth-tone tissues into a semisolid silver chrome matter. I saw a team of little men shaping the matter into a ball. They polished the ball into a perfectly shined chrome sphere that floated in the middle of my rib cage. All the little men looked at their reflections in my chrome sphere. They saw their faces fish-eyed, their body parts closest to the ball magnified. These drapes are horrid, I heard one of them say as he ran his fingers over the rungs of my ribs. Why do the curtains go so poorly with this chandelier? I felt my interiors breathing. As I brought fresh air into my lungs I could feel the chrome ball inside of me quivering.

CONCERNED HUMANS
\\\\\\\\\\\\\\\\\\\

KARL WAS A SNAKE who coiled himself into the shape of a pear and bit the children who tried to eat him. He lived in a tree surrounded by sidewalk cement on a busy block in a big city. He hung from the low swinging branches and wrapped himself into the shape of a fruit. He stuck out his tongue on the top of his coil to give the children who passed what looked like a newly sprung leaf. He shifted color to match the tree. He greened with a perfect speckle. A young boy came up to the pear and stuck out his arm to pick it, and Karl, instead of juicing, revealed his fangs and said, rather boldly, "I love you." And with that the venom entered the boy's veins. Karl lapped up the extra blood and then went back to pretending to be a fruit. Pigeons picked at the dead boy's bones and then water fell from the sky and washed away his remains and police did eventually find the dead boy but nobody suspected a snake, because who would suspect a pear? Also, this was a city, and city people suspect many things, but cuisine, specifically fruit, generally isn't one of them. Time passed and Karl again waited. He bathed in the night and blinked his lashless eyes and whispered sweet nothings to the spiders who wove webs in his tree. The spiders, squirrels, rats, bugs and stray cats that lived on the block conversed with Karl with caution. Karl said things none of them wanted to remember. He said, "That little girl looked really nice in those shorts," and then later "I have always thought I had a specific type of attraction." The spiders, as well as much of the other surrounding urban wildlife, attributed Karl's strange behavior to his foreign origin or perhaps even to some childhood trauma that Karl himself had yet to explain. They resented that he had killed the little boy, inducing an extreme increase of police traffic on their block, but liked the exotic company and, while they condemned his strangeness publicly, many of them privately reveled in it and were thankful that at least Karl was there, doing his fruit-snake thing, adding some amount of diversity to where there had previously been only vermin. An urban pear tree is a rare thing, the spiders, squirrels, rats, bugs and stray cats all recognized, and having a snake to go with the pear tree, especially a snake masquerading as a pear, was a rare thing indeed. Karl had, in fact, come with the tree. A group of concerned humans had imported the tree from outside the city and planted it in a barren square of sidewalk soil to add some green and life to their block, which had previously been thought of only as a block without green and without any real space to do anything but walk through. But now, with the pear tree, people sat on their porches and talked on the street and breathed in the air with such enthusiasm that it was as if prior to the pear tree, the air had not existed at all. This made Karl's job extremely easy. With all the humans huddled to his trunk, gulping down smog, he had more children to eat than he could swallow. When the weather turned warmer and his tree blossomed, this was especially obvious. To his despair, he maybe no longer even needed to pretend to be a pear. This realization was devastating. Karl liked pretending to be a pear. He liked being a pear so much that he identified heavily as an actual pear. Who was anyone to tell him he was otherwise? Karl realized he liked being a pear in the same way that many humans like not just doing their jobs, but being their jobs. Karl was a pear, now and forever, in the same way retired lawyers are always lawyers. Karl meditated on this reality as he saw humans pass. He saw construction workers, teachers, bus drivers and chefs and, very clearly, how some of them were just people who had jobs, but others were people who were their jobs. Was Karl a snake who was a pear? Was he really a pear who only looked like a snake? If you cut him open, what would be within him? Snake flesh bleeding green guts? No. Karl knew what he was. He was certain that within he only held white sugar-filled flesh. Flesh that could be poached or jellied or painted or simply sliced. Flesh, that when children chewed, would sweeten, soften and slide down. Thus Karl started to have fantasies about being eaten. It started out as just dreams but then he started planning to let the next child who tried to eat him do so. "I am done as a snake that looks like a pear," he thought. He thought, "I simply am a poison pear." The squirrels and the spiders on the block all thought Karl was crazy, confused, "hyped up on spring." But Karl went through with it. One morning, a boy about the age of eight came up to Karl, and plucked him from his tree, and Karl stayed put, stayed coiled in his pear-shaped form, and sat in perfect stillness as the boy bit into him, ingested his venom orally, and died on the street with Karl in his palm. There Karl lay, chewed in two, happily being seen and understood as the thing that he was: a poison pear. But wasn't Karl also just a snake? A snake trying to find a way to eat that was respectable, and clever, and allowed a little time to be left over in the evenings so that when the sun set over the urban sky he could chat with his neighbors? In this way Karl was and was not the thing he wanted to be. As his snake blood seeped out of his snake body, the spiders and the squirrels and the bugs and the rats and the stray cats crowded around. They looked at Karl, and they wept for him, and they admired him as the sweet and fleshy product of a tree, as a plant that contains seeds, as a simple food that can be eaten.

FRIED DOUGH
\\\\\\\\\\\\\\\\\\\\\\\\

A PARTICULAR TYPE OF LOVE STORY takes place in twenty-four-hour donut shops. It involves teenagers in a suburb to a great city. It happens slowly, and then quickly. As in, the teenagers have known each other for most of their lives, and they are just people, and then they are something else: they are in love. In the twenty-four-hour donut shop everything looks yellow. The fluorescent lights make the girl's cheeks shiny and pale. In this love story, though, this doesn't much matter. The teenagers are ugly. The girl's hair is cut too short and the boy's hair has grown too long and red dots cross both their forehead, cheeks and chin. The donut shop, too, is ugly. It is rundown and johns come in at 3:00 a.m. and get raspberry creams. However, in this love story this ugliness is the right place for the teenagers to be. The donut shop lets them chip paint off chairs because it is a place where only chipped paint chairs reside. Underneath the chairs there is linoleum and underneath the linoleum is a basement that the teenagers have never seen. Paint peels from the ceiling. The smell of burnt sugar sticks to the teenagers' tongues. Large glops of icing slop fall off old pastries contained in the glass case next to the counter. The wall behind the case was white but has turned a deep cream. An immigrant man works the cash register. One of the teenagers buys a chocolate glaze. This teenager is sixteen, and in twenty-four-hour donut shops all sixteen-year-olds are seen as their own type of criminal. If they haven't stolen something yet, they will. This sixteen-year-old takes three donut holes while the cashier isn't looking. This sixteen-year-old shoves them in his pockets and brings them to the other teenager. The other teenager is fiddling. She has seen the crime and is taken by the fact that someone wants to give her something. Neither of these teenagers is stupid, but they're not smart, either. They are simply half-formed people who are trying to talk to another person and find a way to feel less like there is less in the world and more like there is in fact more. There is more in this donut shop. In this donut shop there are people who sit by themselves late into the night that don't have the kind of itinerary that these teenagers have. There are also people who are mad. A woman in a paisley dress and matted black hair sits in a corner and mutters words about the kinds of ghosts that live in kitchens. The teenagers talk to the woman in the paisley dress and make her mutterings into sentences and then write the sentences down on a piece of paper that they tape inside the establishment's bathroom, right above the sink, so that when someone goes to rinse their hands they read, "I am waiting for you in the sugar bowl and other parts of the pantry." The woman in paisley dress reads the bathroom announcement and walks out the door and past the peeled paint. She waves to the teenagers as she walks down the road, exhaling words as she saunters out of sight. In this donut shop there is also graffiti. It is in the bathroom where the note is, and under the table and on the very plates on which the donuts are occasionally served. The graffiti cusses people and other suburbs that are close to the city and the teenagers feel that they are close to this anger by sitting on top of this graffiti and they like this feeling. They do not scratch anything themselves, however, because right now they are not angry, they are just nervous. Nervous not because they don't know each other, but nervous because the way they thought the world worked has suddenly shifted. It has been shifting in small ways for a long time and the teenagers have grown accustomed to these shifts and have learned to steady their legs and even sometimes predict when these shifts are coming. The boy has learned that his father lies to him. The girl's sister has been going places and doing things that she has not done. This difference in experience has caused their link to shift and the girl and her sister are no longer on the same plane, but rather drifting pieces of land across the stretch of the ocean. Two people that were close but are now apart, and that closeness that was once so present is now simply a mark on a timeline that has been passed. Here, in this twenty-four-hour donut shop, things are shifting too. The teenagers are looking for things, but they're not sure what. They have big fantasies that they think up together and a conception of the world that is wholly wrong, but shared, and that is what makes it real. What these teenagers want more than anything is simply to find another person who wants to experience the world with them, feel the cold of a winter lake or the pain of a cut gained or the thrill of breaking into an abandoned house or, this specific instant: biting into to a piece of fried dough that is not completely good but that is not bad either, it is just the right food to eat because they are in a donut shop. And donuts are food that is good, but not too good, and these teenagers don't need good food right now because right now they are in love, and when in love what one puts in one's mouth never really matters. The teenagers come back to the twenty-four-hour donut shop many times. They drive their suburban station wagons across the wide expanse of lanes and into a part of their city where the donut shop resides. They come to the donut shop late, when their parents are sleeping and when the only people in the streets are the ones who are on trial by society at large. The teenagers crawl in and sit in a booth next to the window where the flashing lights of passing cars and the glow of neon signs reflect off their faces. The girl pulls her legs up to her chest and hugs her knees. The boy's long hair falls in his face when he turns his head to look outside. Seated like this, the teenagers talk to each other, and learn what makes the other feel most strongly that they will never be more than the items they own and the words they say. Then each teenager refutes this feeling, and acknowledges that the other is more than the sum of their actions and possessions, and this gesture is a new gesture and it makes the teenagers feel like more of a whole person than they have previously felt like, as if someone has added sections to their body, filled in gaps and holes and the thin little bits so that they are no longer as see-through as they used to be. Although both teenagers had suspected that this feeling could happen, they are in a giddy space of disbelief at its obvious existence. Another human has come forward and reassured them. This is enough to fall in love, they both agree internally. But the teenagers fall further. Their fall is hurried by their setting. The twenty-four-hour donut shop allows them not only to acknowledge each other as human beings, but to see that there is a place in the world for them and that this place might be together. The teenagers write things and draw pictures. They sketch the patrons' faces on napkins and give them to the cashier. Thus the teenagers win the hearts not only of each other, but also of the people that surround them. This is something new for both of them. These two teenagers are kind and generally all right at talking, but winning hearts is not their specialty. But for some reason, in this donut shop, people like them. They are so young. The teenagers suspect the old drunks see them as children, which the teenagers admit to the drunks, and themselves, they very well might be. And the drunks and the drug dealers and the johns and the women the johns bring with them find them fascinating.

"Ugly children who are in love!" the woman with purple hair whispers to the drunk in the blue jacket. The teenagers suspect that these other people in the donut shop see something of themselves in them. That the john with the funny suit and slouchy eyes and the drunk with missing teeth and gray wiry curls see a small version of themselves when they look at them. And the teenagers like this feeling. They like the feeling of being seen as something other than themselves, and they like the feeling of someone seeing themselves within them. And they also like the feeling of knowing that they could be a drug dealer or a john or a drunk or insane, because that means that their futures are varied, and even if those things are bad at least they are new things, things different from what they know now and things that they cannot possibly foresee. In this twenty-four-hour donut shop, time is a thing that has happened but is, more importantly, something that has not yet come to pass. It is a thing that the teenagers know lay ahead of them, at least much more so than behind. The teenagers look at each other and wrap their legs together around the base of the table. The girl teenager folds her arms in front of her and puts her head on her wrists and falls asleep. The boy teenager looks at her for a long time and is overcome with the feeling of sheer fortune that he has found someone who is willing to speak with him and draw with him and do things with him including doing nothing at all. He looks out the window into the night and sees the sway of the trees planted in the middle of the street. Large redwoods interspersed with sickly palms shake their dried limbs over the cars that speed past them.

The light of the night hovers above the buildings across the road, hanging a haze on to the roof of the single-story structures like snugly fit clothes. The boy teenager continues to look outside and thinks he hears a bird yell from one of the trees in the middle of the street. He cranes his neck and looks for the bird but cannot see it. Looking for the bird makes him sleepy. He puts his head next to the girl teenager's and also falls into a deep lull. In their lull the teenagers wind their arms together and curve into the gray seat of the booth. They lie intertwined, breathing with their eyes closed, letting their minds wander back and forth to each other and then they are both sound asleep, sleeping next to each other like blind newborn puppies, huddled up to the light of the neon signs, blind from the new birth and happy, oh so happy, that they have someone next to them whose eyes are just as wrecked. The teenagers wake in the twenty-four-hour donut shop when the sun comes through the street-facing window and the light turns their table more blue than yellow. They go home to their own beds and then come back to the twenty-four donut shop when light again escapes from the day. In this love story, the teenagers continue in this way. They go places that are not the twenty-four-hour donut shop, but the twenty-four-hour donut shop remains the place that they always go. Bad things do happen to the teenagers, but these bad things happen outside the donut shop and never, ever while the two teenagers are together. In this way, the teenagers become more melded than most people think two people can be, and far more than the teenagers themselves know consciously. In the dawn of the donut shop, the teenagers imagine the rest of their lives together. They do not speak of their imaginings, but rather have a sense of their existence from their mutual way of knowing and the ways in which each of them expresses ideas about the world and the ways in which they believe this world to work. In their discussions about the workings of the world, there is the understanding that they are in the world together, and therefore any understanding of the world they gain is only possible because the two of them are there sitting together, thinking together. And it is only together that they can figure the world out and perhaps even make it yield a small space for the two of them to reside permanently, away from the suburb, away from their families, and in a place that they know nothing about, but simply imagine is a place that will show them more than the place they are currently in. In this way, there is a slight betrayal of the twenty-four-hour donut shop. The teenagers see it as a place they are in now, but also as a place that they will leave, marching through its cranky, squeaking, poor bell door, past the johns and the drunks and the people with madness written all over their faces and into a place that may have twenty-four-hour donut shops that are not this particular twenty-four-hour donut shop, and that, as both the teenagers acknowledge fully, is a truly different thing. However, the teenagers, despite their thoughts of flight, do have a sense of savoring. They know, somewhere in the space between when they fell in love and when they will be older, that this finding of solace and rest and sleep in a store—a place of commerce, a shop where pieces of dough are fried and dusted with sugar—is a special space that they have made, with their thoughts, into more than an area in which people exchange goods for money. In this love story, this twenty-four-hour donut shop becomes them. Because they spend so much time within it, the donut shop builds a replica of itself in each of their souls where, for the rest of the teenagers' lives, they will go in their dreams, and whenever a new possibility, such as new love, presents itself and says to them, "I am here. Let me grow within you," the teenagers will say in their sleep, "Of course. We are here in the twenty-four-hour donut shop, where thoughts can do nothing else but breed." Breed not just thoughts, but ideas and feelings and an aura of humanness that the teenagers, up until this point in their lives, have found nowhere else. In this love story the teenagers will go on to find other people and other places that reveal that nature is an imperfect thing that has a space for them as well as much more. But, it is this particular twenty-four donut shop that offers them this first experience, this first feeling that they are more instead of less. The teenagers come and go, but mostly they stay and sit and eat cinnamon twists and double chocolate éclairs and glazed crullers and pieces of dough filled with a substance called lemon filling that the teenagers acknowledge alludes to the taste of lemon but is probably not actually derived from that exact fruit. Thus the teenagers settle into themselves, and each other, and the people who surround them, and also the people they encounter in spaces outside. In the twenty-four-hour donut shop, they bring things to read and sometimes they read out loud, and once the girl teenager got on a chair and screamed a passage of a book that she thought was more beautiful than anything she had been previously told was beauty. The immigrant cashier clapped and the john in the funny suit had bowed, which was strange to the teenagers, as it was the teenager who had done the reading, not the john. But, in this love story, the teenagers didn't care, because after the reading there was a feeling of all-encompassing joy, like someone had shot lightning through all their hearts and that God was allowing everyone, the john included, to stand there, living, electrocuted in the wake of words that meant something about all of them, and therefore maybe the john had the most right to bow, or at least as much right as the reader, who in this case was the teenager, but in retrospect it seemed as if the entire donut shop had read the passage together, emanating a single sound, as if everyone in the donut shop had composed something collectively, and this was a better feeling for the teenager than the feeling of her just reading alone, so she chose to remember this moment differently than it happened. She remembered the entire donut shop reading the passage in unison, everyone having a copy of the same book, reading from the same page, screaming the words in a perfect chorus, and then, at the very end, the john mounting a chair and taking his bow, a bow that was in truth not only his, but every person's bow who had ever entered a space in their lives where there was no beauty and then beauty was, miraculously, found. In this way, in this particular twenty-four-hour donut shop, in this particular type of love story, there were things that happened that were later misremembered. But most of the things that were misremembered were real, or at least more real than so many other things the teenagers would go on to see crowd the space of time between when they lived and when they ceased to be.

IN THE SOUTH, THE SAND WINDS
ARE OUR GREATEST ENEMY
\\\\\\\\\\\\\\\\\\\

GLEB AND OLEG WERE banished brothers. They lived to-gether in a prison infirmary surrounded by snow. Gleb was a surgeon and Oleg a sculptor. When the brothers were banished, Gleb convinced an officer that in order to be of use, they had to stay together.

"I have bad eyesight," Gleb had said. "And a poor sense of proportion. I need my brother's eyes to make sure I sew things on in perfection."

"It's true," Oleg had said. "Anatomy has never been Gleb's forte."

The officer had squinted his eyes at Gleb and Oleg in

consideration. Oleg was infinitely more handsome than Gleb, but far thinner. How can one work with such a pretty face? Oleg-faced people were never much use anyway.

"Alright," the officer had said. "If you need your brother's eyes, so be it. People often lose limbs around here, so I expect, with the two of you on the job, there to be no excuse for failed attempts at reattachment."

"Thank you," Gleb said. "We'll do just fine."

Gleb and Oleg sat at a desk during the day and slept in the sick beds during the evening. The sick beds were comfy, straw filled-mattresses. The sheets were good, blue wool with stripes. Ten days after their arrival, Oleg took to wearing a nurse's hat that he found under one of the blankets.

"You've always liked looking womanly," Gleb grumbled.

"You're just jealous mom used to let me wear her Sunday dress," Oleg batted his eyes.

As Oleg giggled to himself a man came in the front door with a missing digit. "My God!" Oleg said. "Where is your thumb?"

"No idea," said the man. "One of my prison-mates accidentally lopped it off with a shovel. It took me a good moment to realize it had gotten away. My hand was nearly frozen solid from bricklaying out by the west wing. I had my whole squad looking for it in the snow but we found nothing. White snow, white thumb. A needle in a haystack."

"More like a butter cookie in a pile of powdered sugar!" Oleg exclaimed. "In the south, the sand winds are our enemy," Oleg continued. "But here in the north, our enemy is the snow." Oleg tried to exhibit appropriate bedside manners and show his sympathy for the loss of this man's digit. He was still wearing a nurse's hat and sat down on the side of one of the beds and sighed.

The man looked confused and slightly put out by Oleg's melancholy.

Gleb said, "Well, let's look among the recent corpses and see if we might be able to find something suitable."

In search of a digit, Oleg, Gleb, and the nine-fingered man walked out in to the cold and over to the burial pit. The ground was frozen solid so the corpses lay exposed. Gleb crawled over the dead men, occasionally picking up their hands and examining. He pulled the corpses' fingers apart and tried to look into the muscles of the hands.

"Hold up your hand!" Gleb yelled to the nine-fingered man standing at the edge of the burial pit. The nine-fingered man lifted his four-fingered hand above his head.

"Solidly medium-sized," Gleb said. He kept looking among the corpses until he found a suitable replacement. Then he pulled out his pocket-knife, took the serrated edge, and sawed through the bone.

"Look away!" Oleg screamed and jumped to cover the nine-fingered man's open sockets. "It's like seeing your bride's gown before you are married! Bad luck, bad luck! Give the thumb some privacy, you'll be in union soon enough!"

The nine-fingered man dutifully closed his eyes and was led back to the thumb marriage bed in the infirmary. Oleg tucked him in, read his palm, told him a story, and then put the man to sleep. Oleg dipped a rag in a pot of ether and draped it over the nine-fingered man's face until his breathing was deep and steady.

Gleb came back in soon thereafter. He took the thumb out from his pocket and laid it next to the sleeping man's nub to make sure it fit for size.

"Damn," Gleb said. "I took off the left instead of the right thumb."

Oleg rolled his eyes and stroked the hair of the sleeping patient. Gleb went back out into the cold and then returned promptly with the right thumb.

Oleg looked at the two thumbs on the counter and thought of the now eight-fingered corpse in the burial pit.

"Get the water boiling," Gleb ordered.

Oleg took a pot outside and filled it with snow. He lit the flame on the gas stove and placed the pot to boil. In a matter of minutes the snow melted to water which bubbled over. Gleb took the nine-fingered man's thumb-to-be and plopped it in.

The thumb had been frozen solid so it took a good ten minutes to thaw and become pliable. Once the veins had melted blood started to seep into the water and make it pink. When the blood really started pouring, Gleb fished it out with a serving spoon. He bent the thumb and then straightened it to make sure it was working. After he verified the thumb's suitability he opened many of the drawers to see if he could find some suture needles and stitch string.

"Should we name the thumb?" Oleg asked. Gleb was annoyed with Oleg and his nurse hat, so he didn't respond.

When Gleb finally found the appropriate materials, he went to work. He yanked the nine-fingered man's veins out of his hand and attached them to veins in the corpse thumb. After he was done attaching the veins, he knitted the muscles together, and, lastly, attached the two pieces of flesh by the skin. As the thumb became connected blood pumped into it in earnest. It turned from white to pink and twitched slightly in its sleep.

The nine-fingered man, now ten-fingered mutant, came to and looked at Oleg and Gleb with starry appreciation. He wiggled his new thumb and kissed it to welcome it in.

"You're going to use that thumb for a lot of nasty things," Oleg raised his eyebrows in insinuation.

The ten-fingered mutant man was too grateful to catch the hint of insult. Gleb looked satisfied with the end result. Oleg sang some folk songs to the patient to wake him up and bring him back to his regular self. Oleg and Gleb congratulated themselves on a successful operation and sent their perfect patient back to the barracks.

Within three days' time, word of Gleb and Oleg's surgical magic spread throughout the prison. People made long lines outside the infirmary, and when the officer finally called on Gleb and Oleg to congratulate them on the reattachment, it was too crowded for him to even push himself in. Oleg was on a table demonstrating the latest waltz trends from the Continent. Gleb had diluted some ether with water and was drunk as a newborn bull.

It was then that the officer realized that Gleb and Oleg were basically just having a gigantic party. He was furious, and decided he needed to give them some work, show them who was boss and what they were here for. Determined to prove a point, the officer marched into the barracks and found an innocent old man alone reading the Bible.

"Get dressed!" the officer shouted. "Report to the ninth ward!"

Startled, the old man got up and quickly dressed himself. He shuffled slowly over to the ninth ward where the officer sat and wait. There, the officer took an icepick and gouged out the old man's eye sockets. The old man screamed and fell to his knees writhing in pain. Eyeball flesh oozed out of his face and onto the floor planks.

"Fix *that*, Gleb and Oleg!" the officer proclaimed.

Shortly after the old man's gouging, a prisonmate found the old man comatose on the floor of the ninth ward.

"Help!" the concerned prisoner yelped. "Help! Someone help me carry this old man to Oleg and Gleb!"

Several other prisoners quickly materialized and helped carry the old man's body out through the snow and into the infirmary.

Gleb and Oleg were recovering from an ether binge from the night before and were still slightly drunk. When Oleg saw the old man's eyes he vomited into a cup.

"Ew!" said Oleg.

"My God," said Gleb.

The concerned prisoners and Gleb and Oleg all looked at the old man gravely. Gleb asked to speak to Oleg alone so they could decide what should be done.

"Well," said Oleg. "At least he was an old man who was already mostly dead anyway."

"Fool," said Gleb. "He isn't going to die. The issue is that he'll never again be able to see."

"Well," said Oleg. "What's at stake here?"

"Our pride," said Gleb. "And possibly our standing with the other prisoners. The officer did this to this poor man to show us that we weren't deities."

"What a tiresome thing to try and prove," Oleg said. "If you are asking me to make an ice-sculpture pietà, forget it."

"It is worse than that," said Gleb. "I think we have to figure out a way to make this blind man see."

Wind swung outside the infirmary. For Gleb and Oleg this seemed like it could be the end of the line. But then, Oleg remembered having seen a nervous looking prisoner who slept with a stuffed doll that had glass eyeballs.

"That's it!" Oleg shouted. "What is better than seeing beauty but being beautiful?"

His plan hatched and he shared it with his brother. The two of them reached a consensus for a plan of attack and then asked the concerned prisoner who had brought in the old man to find the nervous prisoner with the doll and steal his beloved figurine.

In the meantime, Gleb prepared the old man's eye sockets. He scooped the remaining eyeball matter out and cauterized the nerves. A calm came over the old man when he realized he was being taken care of and he barely whimpered. When the cleaning was done, the old man blinked his empty sockets in repose.

"The deepest black," the old man said. "Bluer than anything else I have ever seen. Like the depths of the sea."

"How lovely," said Oleg. "It sounds relaxing. Take note, Gleb. If they ever really get ahold of me, be sure to first gouge out my sight."

Finally, the concerned prisoner reentered the infirmary with the doll with the glass eyeballs.

"It's perfect!" said Gleb.

Oleg examined the doll and then took a razor and cut out the glass eyes. While Gleb went to work sterilizing them, Oleg sewed the doll's eyes shut and painted some eyelashes onto its face with coal.

"Now it's sleeping," Oleg whispered to the concerned prisoner who had brought the doll in. "See if you can't find the man who this doll belongs to and return it to him. Tell him the doll told us she was tired of seeing the horrors of this prison. We only took out her eyes on her own request, just following a patient's orders, explain to him. I am sure he'll be quick to understand."

The concerned man looked skeptical about the returning of the doll but hurried away regardless. Gleb had almost finished sterilizing the glass eyeballs and was picking off some stubborn glue.

Oleg turned to the old man on the operating table and said, "The sight this operation is going to restore for you will be slightly different. It will require a bit more imagination than your previous eyes allowed. One could, however, say that you'll have a true artist's eyesight. You'll be able to see the kind of beauty of which I dream. Also, the images these eyes will show you will be closer to godliness. The usual eyes we are born with don't really do us much service in that regard. So, just be aware that these new eyes will give you images that you'll have to see through. Just crack the images you see like an egg and part the canvas."

And with that Oleg leaned in and kissed the old man on the forehead. The old man looked into the space in front of him and relaxed. He blinked his empty sockets in anticipation. The pits of his eyes looked ready for filling and Gleb put on his operating gloves and readied himself to insert the new eyeballs in.

"Alright," said Gleb. "This shouldn't hurt, but let me know if you feel anything."

Gleb took forceps and pulled the right lids of the old man apart.

"Oleg! Grab the ball!" Gleb ordered. Oleg grabbed the glass eyeball and inserted it in. There was a sudden pop and the eye was sucked into the socket. The old man blinked over the glass eyeball and grinned.

"The other one! Quick!" said Gleb. He wanted to keep the momentum going.

When both of the eyeballs were in, the old man sat up and blinked his eyelids over his new appendages.

"Saints," said the old man. "I was blind, but now I can see!"

The old man gripped Oleg's hand and squeezed it in appreciation. "It's how you said it was going to be, my dear fellow. A different type of sight, but perhaps with time, when I learn how to use it properly, it will reveal more than I used to know."

Oleg helped the old man to stand and walked him back to the barracks. When the prisoners saw that Oleg and Gleb had restored the old man's sight they cheered.

"Gods!" yelled one of the prisoners. "True prophets!"

Gleb looked bashful and tried to shake off the compliments over the roar of appreciation. Oleg soaked it up and took a deep, graceful bow.

The officer heard the ruckus from his sleeping quarters and marched over in a huff to investigate. When he arrived at the barracks he found the old man whose eyes he had gouged sitting before him restored to perfect health and cheering. It was as if the gouging had in fact inserted in the old man some renewed youth. The old man's arms were above his head thrusting in celebration. The officer could not look away from the old man's perfect, new blue eyes.

In fear, the officer frantically scanned the barracks and looked around him. In the far corner of the room he spotted Gleb and Oleg being lifted up into a crowd. The prisoners were shouting, "Gleb and Oleg! Gleb and Oleg!" The sound of the prisoners' voices was deafening. The cheers grew louder, and the officer could no longer remember which name belonged to which brother, and whether or not they were two men or two different names for the same.

"Gleb and Oleg!" the prisoners shouted. "Oleg and Gleb! Oleb and Gleg!"

Gleb and Oleg were hoisted by the prisoners up onto one of the rafters where they did a jig and danced with each other. The prisoners continued to cheer and sing. Oleg, being the ham that he was, convinced Gleb to waltz on the rafter and swung him around and dipped him over the edge of a railing. The prisoners went wild and stamped their feet. Oleg winked at the crowd and then kissed Gleb on the lips in mock courtship. Soon every prisoner in the barracks was waltzing in pairs and singing the same tune. The old man, overjoyed by this celebration of his return, threw his long beard over his shoulder and whooped and hollered. His few-toothed grin spread across his wild, well-worn face.

The officer looked on at all of this in the utmost fear and realized that these two brothers were reincarnations of the devil. The officer hurried back to his own quarters where he promptly made a noose, mounted a chair, put his head in the loop of the rope and hung. The officers' eyes bulged out from his head and a red ring of rope burn formed around his collar. He was a very large, fat man, so gravity worked with him and took his life away rather quick.

While the officer hung himself, Gleb and Oleg continued to celebrate their medical successes.

A villager who lived close to the prison overheard the joyous yells and looked into a hole in one of the side planks of the barrack walls. The villager scanned the scene and saw only joyous dancing. The villager even noticed an old man, spry, younger looking than his years, dancing alone. To be in prison, the villager thought, and free of burden! Were all of us to be so lucky!

And with that thought in his mind, the villager walked back to his own home across the snow-filled tundra. He shuffled his feet and carried his heavy load of wood and wool. As he walked, the moon rose above him and a flock of geese gawked, it seemed, directly at him. The space between the villager and the prison widened and snow flurried in quicker circles around him. The wind and the ice deadened the noise that the villager had heard from the prison. From that moment till the end of his trek, the only sounds that the villager heard were simply the noise of the elements hurling things at him. In an attempt to shield himself, the villager pulled his fur hood further over his forehead. To amuse himself, and keep himself from chilling, he tried to sing the barrack jig, "Gleb and Oleg! Gleb and Oleg!" the villager cried. "Gleb and Oleg!" the villager sung and kicked his legs in rhythm. "Gleb and Oleg!" said the villager as he waltzed all the way into the warmth of his wife and his well-cooked dinner safe at home.

PASSING

\\\\\\\\\\\\\\\\\\\\

I HAVE TWENTY-FOUR HAIRCUTS WORTH of grief, twenty-four times since the barber has taken her razor to my nape, eight years, three trims a year, since my husband was taken from me, dragged out into the night and transported by bus or train or foot (I don't even know) to the tundra, some land covered with snow, and if not snow, then barren prairie, where not even the birds know how to survive. My barber cuts the front parts first and then works her way to the rear.

I go in to get a haircut. I see my gray hair fall in snips, clumps of white are strewn across the barber's floor. I see my husband, an inch tall, shoveling the white away, clearing the walkway to his barracks, pushing my wisps of hair aside, out of the way, watch out, I tell him, watch out, another one is falling, another piece of hair coming your way, it's a big one, better move before it falls.

I keep my hair short in a bob with straight bangs that hit just above the eyebrow. It's the same cut I had when my husband went away. But my hair, back then, was black and, of course, now it's gray. Perhaps my gray is a gift from my husband, something stealthily sent to me, some piece of his world, the white snow, that he wants to share with me, and this was the only way he knew how.

I save the hair in jars to document the time passing. Each cut gets its own jar. I built a shelf to house them. The jars spectrum from dark to light, from night to white, from black to the absence of color. The gray-haired jars are kinked so the hair looks larger, like more was cut, but it is just the added volume of the wave. Six, twelve, eighteen, twenty-four, I think those are the appropriate deviations. Those are the years that make sense to group together. Those are the time periods that are easiest for me to see.

I fantasize about emptying the jars on my bed and mixing together all of the colors, making a salt and pepper soup and stuffing all the hair into one grand vessel sealed at the top center. My life in haircuts, my husband's absence in snips, my shelf bowing with the wait of glass jars whose contents are waiting to be combined.

When I see my husband in visions, his hair is long, all the way down to his knees, and his beard erupts from his face, grown past his shoulders and down to his belly, where it matts at the ends. He smiles and his grand beard smiles with him. No time has passed for him. He has no cuts by which to mark the rotations of the sun. His hair will grow long enough till the wardens can fashion it into a noose and then they'll hang him by his own hair on a rafter.

I have asked the camp to send me my husband's hair after they are done with him. I will cut the noose up into individual strands and mix it with my own trimmings and light the pile on fire so our hair burns together in a deep hole I have dug in our backyard in the ground.

MOUTH FULL OF FISH
\\\\\\\\\\\\\\\\\\

MY BLOOD AILED AND I sunk with it. Doctors brought their slow death to me on clean forms. I drove far away to make myself absent. While steadying through Texas, my nose gave in and started to leak. I pulled off the interstate and drove through a town. I blinked twice and was in front of a hospital. The white stucco box building popped out from the surrounding desert red. My sweaty hand greased the door lever open and I spilled out onto the pavement. I blinked twice more and was seated inside. Sterile syringes and bleached seats encased me. A nurse showed me the blood she had wooed out of my arm into a bag.

"I'll be right back," the nurse said. I nodded my support.

The nurse waddled away and my eyes roamed the linoleum interior. The squeak of wheelchairs breached the hush. I was in Balmorhea, a two-spit town between Marfa and Taos where people stop to pump gas. Sunlight dulled the colors at the edges of the floral drapes. I was going somewhere and that somewhere did not end in Balmorhea and that showed through my teeth.

"Frank," my nurse called, "Frank, can I do anything else for you before you scoot yourself back to Moonlight Gems?" I turned my head. I wanted to get a good look at this Frank who was getting special attention from my nurse.

Frank sat in an electronic wheelchair with an oxygen tank attached to the back. Clear tubes ran from the tank up Frank's nose and across his cheeks, giving his smile the added movement of the tubes. A digital voice box was stuck to his throat above his wrinkled Adam's apple.

"I'm good, honey love," Frank gurgled, "I'm all set to go."

Frank's words came out broken like a speaker sunk in a shallow bucket of water. After he spoke there was static instead of silence. He looked over at me from across the hallway and smiled big.

I watched Frank as he moved around the hospital on his electronic wheelchair and bid the nursing staff good-bye. He whispered digital well wishes into their ears and kept smirking with his tubes. He breathed heavy as he maneuvered. I watched the back of his head. He finally made his way to the handicap exit and scooted down the ramp out into the desert.

When my nurse returned, I was informed that my blood and I needed to rest, so I checked into a nearby motel. I closed my eyes and then opened them. I folded my body up and out of bed and looked out the window and then at the TV and then decided I had to walk. A walk, I thought, would do me good. I left my room and went into the night. I walked down the road that was the freeway and passed through Balmorhea by foot. Yellow street lamps gave me a shadow. Light also emanated from a single building. A run-down wood two-story with a generous porch and sign reading "Moonlight Gemstones" that seemed to hum in the night. As I approached the building, the sound grew louder. I walked up the stairs, crossed the porch, and pushed open the swinging door of the rock shop into a bath of light and noise. In a panic I covered my ears. Everywhere I looked there were hundreds of little black machines spinning full force. Going around and around with stones inside them and metal cords running from their bodies into the walls. On shelves, on the floor, hanging from the ceiling. All that registered was a blur. The allusion to an object. The sound deadened the space around my body. I could not hear the sound of my feet walking, the hands on my ears, the regular in and out of breaths. The everyday sounds were missing. These machines, these rock tumblers entering my ears, the sounds they made were incinerating my red blood cells one by one, like birds on a fence. Bam bam. I could feel the liquid inside of myself die.

I tried to configure the meaning of these spinning baskets just as Frank appeared and pulled the plug. Silence descended upon the room like a cloud of black.

"Hey, there, stranger," he smiled at me through his nose tubes. "You like rocks?"

Frank machined his way from behind a desk where he had been hidden and rolled out to greet me.

"Rocks, fossils, dinosaurs—just giving them a good polish while the town sleeps. Come here, let me show you some of the best ones I have. I bet you don't have rocks where you come from."

I followed Frank to a jeweler's desk. He took out a worn velvet tray and a series of stones from a drawer. The sudden silence wrapped us in close. He clicked on a desk lamp.

"See here, see these little veins of red reaching towards the edges? The black circle here at the center—that is how you know it's from Balmorhea. These stones from here, right here from my backyard, go all over the world! People like the red bits, that's why—universal beauty right there, ain't it?"

"I am driving from the East and going West," I said.

Frank's smile dropped slightly at the tips of his mouth and he picked up one of the rocks he had laid on the tray. His neck was stiff and couldn't move much so instead of leaning in to tell me his secrets he stretched his hand out from his body and lifted his arm sagging with skin up towards me.

I looked down at Frank's wheelchair. It was a sophisticated machine. On the right arm there were remotes and controls and a small red button under a clear plastic box. Frank flicked the box open, poised his finger above the red button, winked at me, and said, "That's how I send off my torpedoes."

I smiled.

"You want the world tour?" he asked.

I nodded.

"I have remote-control everything," he beamed and scooted around the space. "All the counters are low so I can reach them in my chair."

All the surfaces were coated with grime because Frank couldn't clean.

"I sleep in the back of the shop," he said. "Pull that curtain aside."

Past the curtain was a fancy mechanical bed.

"Damn good bed," Frank said. "Beds like that cost more than a good pick-up truck."

"I'll bet."

"Have you seen the springs?" Frank asked me. "They are just up the road. You could carry me and we could go."

It was night and the air was hot and swimming in a spring didn't sound crazy.

"They're world-renowned, these springs. Concrete man-made sides keep the water in a large spring-fed pool. But the bottom is raw rock, just regular Texan granite. It's deep in parts and during the day or by the light of the moon you can see all the fish and the spring creatures swimming at the bottom. They'll brush up on your legs, these fish, and swim in between your toes and, if you stand still gaping long enough, the little ones will even swim in your mouth."

Frank's eyes were wet and I couldn't tell if it was because he was excited or because he had a leaky eye.

He showed me how to unharness him from his chair.

I hoisted him up. I carried Frank to the springs first like a child and then over my back like a sack of rice. Carrying a man like that makes you feel like you are worth something. Walking was the only way to get there and I was glad for it. We were in a jungle of desert, cactus and thirsty-looking trees getting thicker around us as I pushed on. Frank's oxygen tank weighed heavy on my left hand. My right hand kept Frank balanced on my shoulder. He wheezed into my ear, the sound of his breath as close to life as a recording of waves crashing on a beach. Frank and me, we are our own machine right now, I thought. We are going to make it to this spring and let fish swim in our mouths.

Holding Frank in my arms, his oxygen tank hooked on my side—heavy and making me slow—I wondered how far I had to climb. The heat crept up through my feet as he urged me on. I could see where we were headed. Pavement turned to gravel and I struggled to keep our balance. Frank was wheezing in my arms, yelling at me through his voice box, making me believe this was the last thing I was going to do and if I didn't make it, goddammit, we were all going to stop breathing and die.

When we got to the springs, I put Frank at the base of a tree. I removed my shoes and tested the water with my foot.

"It's how I told you it was going to be," Frank said. He smiled his big gaping smile, his mouth expanding cheek to cheek, his tubes lifting up with joy.

He looked up at the moon and the bright stars. Something flew overhead. There was Frank. Sitting at the base of a tree, his head stretched back, his trachea facing me like a little puckered mouth. I placed his oxygen tank between his knees. It rested there like a sleeping child.

"I like the way you look," I said. "I like the way you look with that tank between your knees."

His head came back down, chin stiff again, his teeth covered by his upper lip, "Five minutes and I'll get rid of this damn thing. I'll catch my breath and then you can carry me in."

I took off everything but my underwear and jumped in the spring. I could feel the nature in the water but I wasn't sure exactly where. The smell, perhaps. The water reeked of life and mold and rot. The moon put silver scars on the surface of the water. I waited for the fish to nibble my legs but none came.

"You lied, Frank," I said. "No fish in this spring—just a fancy granite bottom."

Frank stood, which was something I had not yet seen him do. He pulled the tubes out from deep within his nose and placed them on the tank. He teetered there unoxygenated for a moment, long enough to make me wonder if he was going to topple over. I heard the steady rhythm of his voice box breath radio in and out. Slowly he undressed. I tried not to watch but his old broken body backlit by the desert moon held my eyes. His shirt crinkled off and then his pants. He wore white military-looking underwear.

"Come here," Frank croaked. "I might be standing but I sure as hell can't walk!"

I swam to the side and pulled myself out of the water.

Up close Frank's body looked like a misshapen piece of fruit. I stood next to him.

"You're short."

"I shrunk," Frank replied in the dark. His pecs sunken into his chest, his belly swollen, his paper skin melting off his bones, "We don't have all night. Carry me to the side of the pool."

I lifted him up, his atrophied legs draping over my elbow, and placed him down on the edge. I swung his feet into the water slowly, his mouth making an O upon entry.

"I haven't taken a bath in years," Frank looked at me and smiled. "Get in so you can lift me in after you."

I hopped back in the water and faced Frank. I put my hands on his ribs and braced myself to lift his weight when he croaked, "Stop!"

Frank brought his hand to his neck and made an unscrewing motion releasing the microphone that he spoke through. He put his voice box to the side of him, a couple feet away from the edge of the spring. Frank spoke again but said something I couldn't understand. His voice was small. He beckoned me closer. He pulled air with his hand in the direction of my head.

"Closer," he mouthed.

When his lips reached my ear the wind between our bodies beat louder than his breath, that small sliver of life that pulsed through him, somehow keeping his heart beating, his lungs inflating with the rest of the desert.

"I have to be careful," he heaved, "of getting water in my neck."

With that hard *K*, I heard him and I pulled away and looked at the gaping, sagging hole that he spoke out of. Through the opening in his neck, I saw the muscles in his body and I stiffened.

Frank breathed and looked at me and said, "I am ready now. Bring me in."

Without his voice box, Frank talked to me in mouth movements and motions. We were lucky the moon was so bright or I wouldn't have been able to see his words.

"What's wrong with you?" Frank asked, "What do you have that is so bad?"

"Something domestic," I said.

"You're awful young,"

"Is there an age where your body is allowed to start hating you?"

"You think my body doesn't hate me?"

"But, look at you," I was angered, "My body has no right."

"Did they take a bag of blood out of you here in Balmorhea?"

"Yes, that's why I stopped. I knew I had to get my skin around a needle."

"Ain't that the worst," Frank said.

I looked up at Frank sitting on the side of the spring, his legs dangling in the water, his head tilted slightly back and his neck hole sagging. I looked at Frank and looked at the stars and imagined all of the stars gathering in the center of the sky and then funneling down into Frank's neck hole. I looked for holes on myself. Places where stars could gather and enter into me. There were just the usual ones. If the stars were going to funnel anywhere it would be into Frank's neck.

"What do you think of this hole?" Frank whispered, "You don't have one too?" He was trying to make me laugh.

"Come on, in we go." I was already in the water. I put my hands under Frank's armpits and pulled up. His skin slipped out from under my hands and I was afraid it was going to rip. I tried again and retightened my grip further inside of his arms and pulled up, this time, up and forward. His body lifted off the concrete side and fell into the water. I still had a hold of him. The two of us were wavering like a pair of leaves. I watched for a sign that I could let go. He lifted his arms to the sky and my hands slid off him, his skin dripping from my fingertips. I tried to look away, but I had to keep checking that he was still there, breathing OK, doing his stretching thing.

His movements were giddy. The water took away his weight and let his bones float. While he was doing his movements, I swam over to the other side. It was quite large. There were several alcoves that jutted out from the main spring that looked like natural made hot tubs. We had entered through one of these slight curves. I ducked my head under water in each one. In some, the moon shone bright, and I could see the bottom clearly. Others were dark. The granite shifted under my feet and I realized I might cut myself. There must be some razor-sharp rocks beveled to a slice. In the dark, Frank wouldn't even see the blood leaking. No one would know what happened till

morning when they found Frank wheezing short of oxygen in a spring of my blood, my corpse peacefully floating with the breeze and mixing with the pine needles on
the surface.

I looked back at Frank from across the spring, but I
couldn't see him. I looked harder into the dark, but still no
figure appeared. In a panic I got out and ran to the other
side where Frank had been. I dripped on the concrete still
hot from the heat of the day and looked at the dark that
had swallowed him. Over in a corner I saw bubbles, big
bulbous bubbles, rising up. I prepared to jump in and pull
Frank out, to take my mouth and put it on his neck hole
and breath into him inflating him like a balloon. But as I
approached I saw Frank smiling at me under the water.
He raised and lowered his eyebrows in a playful way. He
was breathing bubbles out of his neck hole, spewing them
in a pattern, listening to the sounds they made and seeing how many bubbles he could blow before he needed
to come back up for air. He finally surfaced, took a deep
breath, and ducked back under. Beneath the water he was
spotlit by the moon. He tilted his head back, and for a moment I was sure that all of the stars in the sky were going
to gather above him and funnel into his neck. He looked
at me and tilted his head back again, his neck hole open
wide. A single bubble emerged, birthed out of him and
bloomed on the surface of the water. Frank birthed three
more bubbles out of his neck hole. Then five. And then it
was a volcano of bubbles on the surface of the water and
Frank popped back up gasping for air, smiling. He looked

at me and winked and said in his small voice that may have only been him mouthing the words, "Didn't even know I could do that."

"You lied, Frank," I said. "I don't see any fish."

"They're here," I thought I heard him say. He beckoned me with a hand motion to reenter the water.

I slid back in and looked around at my feet, at Frank's feet. Suddenly out of the edge of my eye, I thought I saw a fish. A small black zinger no bigger than my smallest finger. I pointed and Frank nodded. The fish escaped my eyes and then reentered my vision. I stuck my hand under the water and opened my palm towards the sky. There were about three feet between my palm and the surface. I waited. I closed my eyes and tried to feel the fish swimming over my palm. I waited for the feathers of movement. None came. I opened my eyes and looked over at Frank. He had his head half in the water and his mouth open. His eyes were looking straight ahead, not at the water or the sky, but ahead of him at some faraway tree. I didn't move. And then it was in. Frank shut his mouth, his eyes wide, and pulled himself over to the side of the spring and spit it out. The fish flopped there on the cement looking like a glass toy. It was shiny and black and pretty. I realized it was dying and made a move to put it back in the water but Frank stopped me with his bony hand and mouthed, "Let it die."

Its flipping got more violent, and the fish's mouth gaped, opening and closing for the water, but no water came. I looked far out into the desert, away from the fish, and the place on the pavement where the fish had been flapping went silent. I left Frank where he was and got myself out of the spring. I didn't need to look at Frank or at the fish. I could have just left him there in that pool. I could have walked back to town in ten minutes and who knows how long Frank would have to wait un-oxygenated in that spring. Maybe it was closed tomorrow. I hoped it was.

I put on my pants and my tennis shoes and wore my shirt around my head like a turban until my chest dried. It was clear to me that I didn't know Frank at all. He waited on the side for me to pull him out. He was resting his head on his crossed forearms up on the cement surrounding the spring. His cheek was on his wrist and he looked posed like a beauty queen. I wouldn't have been surprised if he batted his eyes at me. That would have been something that Frank would have done. I tried to forget the dead fish. I didn't look at it or acknowledge it was there. The horizon got yellow. I lifted Frank up out of the pool and let him dry off with his feet in the water. He twisted his voice box back on and cleared his electronic vocal cords. I was glad that the hole in his neck was covered again. I'd had enough.

I helped him to stand. He dripped on the cement.

"Get me my tank."

I pulled it from the place it had been resting in the dirt and handed him his tubes. He put them back up his nose and around his face and breathed in and visibly got larger with the oxygen coming into him. His white army boxers clung to his legs and his balls, and he looked like the least human thing I had ever seen. There he was: wet, slick with scales, shaped like a rotten pear and that machine erupting out of his face. With the morning light, his body showed skin spots with growths and moles and brown patches and purple subterranean veins.

We exited the same way we came. I carried Frank, the both of us still dripping, through the desert path and back to the Balmorhea strip. The sun rose behind us and we traveled wet and broken in the middle of the street.

"How do you think we look?" Frank said.

"Good," I said. "We look good."

As we walked, I saw Frank and me shoved in the mouth of a doctor, reclining under a giant tongue, living in pools of spit together, Frank's tubes anchoring him to a cavity-ridden molar further back in the doctor's jaw. I saw us playing cards under the palate and popping canker sores for fun and harvesting dead taste buds for a grill we had set up near the esophagus, me swinging on the tonsils like a tube swing over a river, pumping my legs, pushing my momentum back and forward, back and forward out of the doctor's mouth and onto the hard cement below.

WHAT GIRL BUILT
\\\\\\\\\\\\\\\\\\

GIRL ON BOAT, boat covered in ice, ice holds boat in place.
Letter is delivered to boat. Girl comes out of boat and skis
north to direction from which letter came. World is cold
and snow creates dunes that are blown about by wind.
Girl's hands are covered by leather gloves and girl's face is
covered by cloth but she is cold and cannot breathe well,
ice closes in. Girl must keep skiing because ice is following. If ice catches girl, she will be limp in ice's grasp and
disappear into snow she is passing. A small domed stone
cottage with a thatched roof comes into girl's view and
is illuminated by lantern hanging outside. Stone chimney
rises up out of cottage roof and smoke rises up out of stone

chimney. Arched wood door opens and girl sees girl's aunt. Aunt wears apron and rushes to greet almost frozen girl and pulls her inside aunt's cottage of warmth and food. Aunt leads girl down spiraling stairs underground to large banquet table where all of girl's family sits and eats. Girl looks around table and discovers mother, father, uncle, sister, grandmother, cousin, cousin, cousin. Girl looks at mother and says,

—Mother, I got your letter, where is Iver?

Family stops eating and uncle stands and opens mouth to let out words. Uncle sits back down and turns to aunt. Girl stays standing and looks at family. Girl is still mostly frozen and cannot move her limbs in the manner that she normally moves them. Ice has melted into her and her scalp is wet. Girl is hot and sweats but is still numb. People start to eat again. Mother gestures to girl to sit next to mother on wood bench that faces large banquet table but girl's eyes widen. Cousin looks at girl and says,

—Come sit—

But girl interrupts cousin and screams,

—WHERE IS IVER.

Girl's mouth is taut and she starts to shake and her teeth make sounds against each other. Grandmother stands up from table, which is hard for grandmother, and whispers,

—Girl, you are not well. You have traveled far. Let me walk you to a bedroom where you can rest your head.

Girl stays standing, shaking and yells at mother about how mother never, never tells the truth in letters. Grandmother hooks girl's arm and leads girl away from banquet table, down another flight of stairs, farther underground into the earth, into a warm small circular bedroom. Bedroom has fireplace with fire and in center of room is bed with many piles of quilts. Girl collapses on bed and puts head in hands and girl's back heaves up and down with sobs of heavy breath. Grandmother leaves girl on bed and shuts door. Alone on bed, girl shakes harder. Girl rocks back and forth until girl has used all of girl's breath. Fire is warm and girl is very hot. Girl stands and moves to door and pulls lock in place to bolt door shut. Girl stands in middle of room and takes off all of girl's clothes. Girl falls to her knees. There on all fours the ground is close. Girl's braid swings back and forth in front of her face. Girl closes girl's eyes and reopens them. Girl closes them again, keeping them shut. Girl sits back on her calves and puts her hands together in her lap. The dirt floor is cold. Girl is sitting on the floor. Girl opens her eyes. There is Iver—across from her on the floor. Iver looks at girl without interest. Iver says,

—Cousin, you have come to visit.

—Yes!

Girl says,

—Yes! My mother wrote and told me to come. Iver— Iver, you look so well!

Iver stays sitting. Iver does not come close to girl. Iver yawns.

—Cousin,

Iver says,

—Cousin—will you build me a chair?

—Iver, what kind of chair would you like me to build you?

—A good chair,

Iver says,

    —Made out of wood and without any nails. Just joints.
I need enough chairs to fill the room.

    —Iver, that is a lot of chairs.

Girl says,

    —Did you bring me a hammer and axe?

    —Yes of course, cousin. Look to your left, you'll find
your hammer and axe.

Girl picks up hammer and axe and walks to pile of wood
between Iver and her. Dirt walls of room expand out re-
vealing many piles of wood and many tools. A domed ceiling rises and girl sees she will need many, many chairs to
fill the room. Girl bends and begins to build. A thing is
built from the things around her and girl says,

    —Iver, I have finished my first chair!

Iver is napping, curled on the floor, his hands under his
head. Girl goes over to Iver and shakes him,

    —Iver, Iver please wake up. I have made you a chair.

Iver opens his eyes and yawns,

    —Cousin, yes, cousin. You have made me a fine chair.
Thank you. To whom will this first chair belong?

    —This chair is yours. The second will me mine. The
rest are for the guests.

    —Cousin, you have much work to do. The night is old.

    —I will work fast.

Iver sits in his new chair and naps some more. Girl makes
chair after chair. As the sun rises girl finishes her hundredth chair. Girl looks around for Iver, to show him the
hundredth chair. The chairs are everywhere—lined up in

the room in neat rows. She has lost track of Iver in this big room.

   —Iver!

Girl yells,

   —Iver—there are many chairs!

Girl walks down rows. Girl looks under chairs. Girl stacks chairs up to the ceiling to make a mountain of chairs. Girl climbs mountain. The rungs of the chairs are slippery on her bare feet. At the topmost chair, girl puts hand to brow and squints for sight of Iver. Girl sees Iver, bathed in the new day, stretched across several chairs in the far reaches of the room. Girl yells,

   —Iver, I built you your chairs!

Iver twitches slightly in his sleep but does not wake. He turns, readjusts himself on his bed of chairs. Girl yells again, her hands cupped around her mouth. Girl is yelling naked on this mountain of chairs, chairs are shaking beneath her feet, her feet slip on the topmost chair and girl falls to the dirt floor.

CLAMOR
\\\\\\\\\\\\\\\\\\\

THE MEDIUM'S HOME WAS a double-wide trailer inside the Willamette National Forest. She lived in a part of the woods that got very little sunlight except in pronounced shafts that looked like lightning rods shot through the dense foliage of tall Douglas fir trees. Immediately surrounding the medium's trailer was a ring of fragrant Oregon red cedars. For extra income, the medium harvested bits of the bark and sold it in baggies online to urban hippies who liked making homemade incense and potpourri.

Saturdays the medium held group communications with dead people. Sundays, she held group communications with deceased pets, mainly cats. The second Saturday in September the medium had a good showing: three seventy-and-over women from Bend proper (Lillian, Phyllis, and Carol), one of whom had brought her two teenage granddaughters (Izzy and Olivia), a fifty-something married couple from Portland (Anna and Cliff), and a single just-over-puberty crew-cut-clad man (Sam). Eight total. She told herself she could feel their collective energy, so she began.

Everyone sat in white folding chairs in a circle in her living room. An afternoon chill had most people in at least two layers. The medium had a silk white cloth wrapped around her head as a headband.

"A moment of silence," she said. And everyone was still. She held out her hands, one to each side, and the people joined hands and touched each other's fingers lightly to form a connected circle. The two teenage granddaughters fidgeted a little in their seats and looked at each other. If the medium noticed their skepticism she didn't say a word.

"A man in a lab coat," the medium said.

"Is he wearing tennis shoes?" said Lillian, one of the retiree Bend women.

"No," said the medium. "He is only wearing socks."

"It's Roger," said Phyllis, one of the other Bend women. "My dead dermatologist. He was into the whole barefoot thing. You know, how it is healthier to stand and run and balance in your bare feet and in his office he only wore those little slippers with the separated toes."

In addition to having a dead barefoot dermatologist, Phyllis also had a husband, who was at home watching daytime television, and two children and several grandchildren, who lived far away. Phyllis enjoyed being in groups and participating in things with other people, which in the past had made her an ardent churchgoer. Mimicking the actions that she saw other people perform gave her a great deal of comfort. She liked knowing what she was supposed to do and then doing it. Like how after church you are supposed to stand outside and drink coffee and eat donuts, and all you have to do is eat and drink, and then you have done what you are supposed to do so that when you run into people at the grocery store they wave to you and respect you and know that you are a respectable person who belongs to a group. When her children had been young, she was very involved in the PTA and the local women's club and ran a lot of bake sales and Christmas caroling drives, although she was never particularly good at cooking or singing or any other craft. Which was part of what brought Phyllis into the medium's trailer. One of her friends from the Bend gardening club, Lillian, was evangelical about genealogy and was excited about connecting with her dead relatives who had homesteaded on the Oregon coast many generations before. So Phyllis came to the medium's house as a follower, as an eager friend open to seeing people pop out from the afterlife, and she was desperate to share this experience with Lillian and the rest of the ladies from the gardening club, because her greatest fear, the one that came to her late in the evenings, was that she had no true friends and that the friends she did have talked about her meanly. She strongly remembered her mother telling her when she was a teenager, "Don't worry so much about having friends in high school. People grow out of their cattiness. Wait until you're older. People will accept you." This Phyllis had found to be wholly untrue. People, regardless of age, were always interested in group-forming. Phyllis felt her life was one long failed attempt to not be left out. So when Lillian had seductively suggested the visit to the medium's house, Phyllis had immediately agreed because it was an easy way to be included and one more Saturday she didn't have to spend alone with her dreaded husband, and this was why she was so eager to claim the first dead spirit as her own—to show Lillian that she was willing and adventurous and able to do anything, and that she was a very good friend who could be trusted to go on other fun outings down the line. When she had gotten in the car over an hour ago, as soon as she had departed from Bend proper, she had made up her mind that she would see a ghost and that was that. When she claimed Roger, her dead dermatologist, everyone looked startled but she was unabashed.

"What does he want?" Phyllis asked the medium. "I don't think I ever paid my last bill."

The medium looked calmly into the space in the middle of the room. She squinted her eyes and said, "He wants you to know it's fine," which seemed to satisfy Phyllis who smiled wildly and mumbled "Thank goodness!" and looked over to Lillian for approval which Lillian did not give.

"He's walking away," said the medium. "And now he is coming back again. With a child. A small child who looks to be about four or five. He doesn't know the child. He's just helping her. It's a little girl. He's carrying her. Now he's leaving again so it's just the little girl."

"Oh my God," said Anna, the wife from the Portland couple. She shook slightly as her husband, Cliff, held her hand. Her eyes were big and wet and her mouth was open.

"Anna, please," said Cliff.

"Is she yours?" said the medium.

"Yes, she is," said Anna, almost screaming. Cliff looked down into his lap.

"I think there is something wrong with her ear," said the medium. "Something on the side of her head."

"She was crushed in an elevator shaft," said Anna. "We lived in an old house with a grocery dolly. She liked playing in spaces where she wasn't supposed to be."

"How long has she been dead?" said the medium.

"Twenty years," said Cliff. He was dry-eyed. Confused, mostly. Trying to figure out the best way to handle his wife.

Anna felt her body turn warm and then cold again, as if Wilma, their dead daughter, had come over and sat on her lap and started grabbing at Anna's hair the way she always had. It had been so long since Anna had seen Wilma. She'd been gone four times as long as she had lived. When Wilma died Anna could feel her presence palpably. She could feel Wilma around the corners, yelling out the window, playing with her stuffed dog, sitting quietly watching television, crawling into bed between her and Cliff. It was impossible for Wilma not to be there so she was there for a very long time, even after they moved houses, even after they had Gabriel, their son. Anna thought of Wilma like a type of weather, like a freeze that had set in on their lives for several years and then lifted, leaving them chilled and disoriented and confused. Wilma was a child. She had only ever been a child and she would be one forever, which terrified Anna and made Wilma seem less like she had ever been a human and more like she had always been an angel that Anna had, unforgivably, let slip through her fingers and die. Anna's sister, Pat, used to tell her on the phone, joke with Anna when Wilma was crying lots in the middle of the night and Anna and Cliff were just young fresh parents. Pat would say, many years Anna's senior, "Honey, your only real job at this point is to just keep her alive." And Pat would laugh because it was a joke, and keeping someone alive was supposed to be an easy thing to do, but it turns out, in Wilma's case, it was not easy, and it did not get done. So that when the funeral happened and Pat flew in from Baltimore she could not look Anna in the eye because she knew that the words she had said on the phone all those years that were supposed to be words of sisterly comfort were stuck in Anna's head and they would not, no matter what Pat said, be able to get free. In the medium's house, deep in the woods away from their pretty Portland home, Anna knew Cliff, her husband, was miserable, but she did not care because after Wilma died, she had learned to be selfish with her feelings and ask for what she wanted with a sense of conviction that she never used to have. She wanted to go to the medium and go they did, because she had asked Cliff with the kind of brokenness in her voice that reminded him that she had been the one who had found Wilma's body crushed in the dolly shaft, Wilma's head smashed, her skull cracked open, her stuffed dog in hand, blood leaking out of her left ear and through a fissure in the top of her head.

"She wants to stay," said the medium. "She has something in her hand. She'll stay until they all have to go away. Is that alright?"

Anna nodded while Cliff stayed silent. Phyllis, who was sitting next to Anna, reached out her arm to offer a comforting hand.

Cliff felt as he had felt since Wilma's death: completely useless. Half of his life had passed in this way. It was a wonder that he and Anna were still together, that they had a son, Gabriel, who was at all able to comprehend them, his grief-ridden, broken parents who were continually haunted by the death of a sister he had never met. When Cliff looked at Anna, he saw Wilma, which made things both harder and easier—harder to forget and easier to remember. He'd been better than Anna at everything in regards to parenting. He'd been better than her at taking care of Wilma and he was better than her at watching Wilma die. And he'd been better than her at having another child, Gabriel, and caring for him, which all contributed to Cliff's belief that there are some people who are better at not being broken, and that his quick tools to repair people, to keep him and Anna together, were a special gift. He had bouts of impatience with Anna, but he learned to leave her alone. He believed much could be said for letting people be. If Anna woke up crying, especially when Gabriel was young, Cliff took off work and got Gabriel out of the house and didn't come back until late in the evening where they always found Anna asleep, no sign she had ever left their bed. So although Cliff was certainly not interested in psychics or the future or in meeting Wilma in some half-dead form, he had gone willingly to the medium's house because it was something that his wife wanted to do and he thought he could handle whatever was going to happen, which it turned out, as he watched Anna cry in the folding chair next to him, he maybe could not.

"She's sitting at your feet," said the medium. "Her head is smudged around the edges so she goes kind of in and out. Now she is using her toy as a pillow. I'll let her rest there and we'll move on."

Anna looked down at her feet as if her eyes could rip into an opening. Cliff tried to look anywhere else but there.

"A young woman," said the medium. "With long blond hair."

Nobody said anything.

"My sister had long blond hair," said Phyllis.

Lillian looked at her menacingly, a look that anyone with any sensitivity knew was a request for Phyllis not to speak.

The young crew-cut clad man, Sam, still sat alone, silently, directly to the medium's left. He looked patient and calm, as if waiting for a bus that he was very sure would come on time.

"Maybe she's got the wrong address," said the medium. "Or, she could be a spectral projection of an earlier, younger version of the deceased—a younger version of an elderly loved one who died."

Carol, one of the Bend women from the garden club, the one who brought her two granddaughters, thought the spirit might belong to her but didn't say anything. She didn't say anything not because she was embarrassed or scared or superstitious, she just didn't really want to talk to the person who she thought it might be—her best child-hood friend, Alice, who had grown up with her in Kansas and gone to college and become a hippie and overdosed on heroin when everyone was doing it and nobody really even knew what it was. As girls, Alice had always been prettier than Carol. Carol's mother used to fawn after Alice and her long blond hair and loudly tell Carol that Carol should eat less and be more demure and Carol mistakenly thought that maybe being a girl now was easier, or at least easier than when she had been growing up in Kansas, and chastised for her size eight frame. Carol tried to imagine what Alice would look like now, old and strung out, missing all her teeth and with yellow fingernails and wrinkly skin. It wasn't really fair, Carol thought, that Alice's ghost would get to stay young forever. She hoped it wasn't Alice, but someone else's fantasy, someone else's dead friend or relative wandering in to find them, or that none of it was real and there was, in fact, no one there.

"She's beckoning to someone else," said the medium. "A group of young men."

Her herd of ever loyal lovers, thought Carol.

These are the people I have killed, thought Sam, the crew-cut clad man.

"They're a group of brothers, I think," said the medium. "But they're not speaking English. Maybe that's why they need the young woman here. She's relaying information for them. One moment please. Please be quiet while I try to go in."

Lillian shifted in excitement that they might be her immigrant homesteading relatives.

Then it was very quiet and Carol's youngest granddaughter, Olivia, listened to the squirrels running up the trunk of the cedar trees and watched the way the light caught on the polyester curtains, emanating an orange glow, and the way the medium's house looked so plastic and crooked and temporary, as if it had been made to be overtaken by nature and its flimsy architecture would yield to the trees and the vines and the animals and the dirt at the slightest push.

Lillian, the master of the garden club, head honcho retiree, most beautiful out of all her Bend friends, the type of mature woman who looked younger than her age and would have been a perfect candidate to advertise expensive eye cream, waited gleefully. Here they were, she thought. Those boys have come to tell me I am the true daughter of their land. Because this was the narrative that she liked to tell herself, that she was of ancient Oregon stock, and before that strong French peasants, who all had good heads on their shoulders and success written on the insides of their wrists. It gave her a sense of authority, this lineage, which she liked telling people and most people, especially old people, found it an interesting narrative, one that checked all the right American boxes, but her friend Carol's granddaughters, who were visiting from Seattle, had found this narrative, which they had been told on the drive down, entirely boring and despicable, especially the older teenage granddaughter, Izzy, who couldn't help thinking that for all old peoples' whining about children being stuck in their computers, that it was the older people who were the ones usually trapped in their own world, trapped in their made-up self-constructed narratives, not the youth. It was the older people like Lillian and her Grandma Carol and most well-off retirees that just told the same origin stories over and over again regardless of whether or not they were even true.

And the stories always helped them. Like Lillian's story about her dumb French ancestors. The story made Lillian seem both sophisticated and exotic and American and established to her garden club friends.

Izzy knew what Lillian was up to when she convinced her grandmother, Carol, and their neurotic friend Phyllis, to go to the medium's house and connect with the dead. This whole thing, this whole trip from Bend, was about Lillian's narrative, what made Lillian look good and posh and fun.

People never change, thought Izzy. Having friends is always an act of competition and mock compassion. Her poor daffy grandmother Carol was no better off than her little sister Olivia on her first day of the eighth grade. Izzy thought of Carol, her grandmother, dressed in Olivia's Catholic school uniform and laughed a little in her head.

Everyone ignored Anna and Cliff, the crying Portland couple, who had already found what they came here to get.

The crew-cut-clad man, Sam, startled everyone when he asked, "What language are they speaking?"

"The foreign brothers?" said the medium. "I can't tell."

"Can you ask them?" said Sam.

"Let me try to ask the woman if she knows," said the medium. "She seems more receptive."

"What are they wearing?" said Sam, quickly, with more than a hint of impatience.

"One moment," said the medium. "I am looking. You know it's not easy to hear what they're saying. It's like looking through a sand storm and trying to hear above the blows of the wind."

The only dead person Izzy knew with long blonde hair was a girl named Felicia whose mother had been a farm hand in Fresno and breathed in all the pesticides during her pregnancy that had likely left Felicia ridden with childhood cancer and dead. After Felicia lost all of her hair their sophomore year of high school Felicia wore a long blond wig which her close friends braided at lunch and put plastic clips in like they were signing the cast of a broken bone. Izzy didn't know Felicia well. She was a friend of a friend. They had gone to the same parties and known who each other were, but when Felicia entered her last stay at the hospital, Izzy did not visit. In this way, Izzy thought of Felicia's death like something tragic she had witnessed on television, something she had seen and had known was bad, but not something that really caused her any real emotional pain. After Felicia had died, Izzy had purchased and worn a big oversized T-shirt that said RIP FELICIA and had a big, color, fuzzy-framed, mall photo of Felicia's face in the blonde wig screen printed on the back.

Izzy did not speak out loud her thought that the unclaimed spirit at hand might be Felicia, because Izzy did not believe in spirits. Being a witch, however, was a fashion aesthetic that Izzy could relate to, so she eyed the medium's silk headband enviously and wondered if she might be able to find it somewhere online where similar ones were sold.

In contrast to Izzy's rejection of the medium's communications, Olivia found that every moment that passed inside the medium's house she was more fascinated. Fascinated not because she believed any magic was really taking place, but because the way people were claiming the dead as the medium roll-called out their features was so bizarre. It reminded Olivia of the time her cousin, Lisa, got married and threw her bouquet out into a crowd of women who all jumped at the same time to catch it, and then screamed and laughed when they did, as if they had won something, which Olivia knew they had, or at least knew what the whole thing meant, impending proposal and so on, but that wasn't what had interested her about the event. What got her watching at Lisa's wedding was the clamoring and the way the crowd shifted when the bride swung left or right. "There it goes," Olivia remembered thinking when Lisa finally threw it. The medium's house was like that. Only everyone got a bouquet.

"No one thinks the blonde girl is here for them?" repeated the medium.

"You weren't able to find out what language the brothers are speaking?" said Sam.

"It's not a language I know," said the medium. "Maybe it's ancient."

"How much do you know about languages?" said Sam.

"Not a lot."

Sam was visibly annoyed by this answer, but his general cool did not waver. Olivia looked at him and realized he was probably in the Army. He had the haircut and clean shaven face for it, and presented himself in a conservative way that showed he was at once used to being told what to do and cared very little for the world that took place outside his own head. Also, there were a lot of young Army men in these parts of Oregon, Olivia knew. Young men who never graduated from high school, or just barely— young men who were looking for something commendable to do.

Olivia, the youngest in the trailer by three years, thought that everyone's faces looked eager. That Anna and Cliff even, despite being settled into mourning, looked attentive and present, and Lillian impatiently awaiting the arrival of her dead relatives, and Phyllis panting quietly in attention, and Izzy and her Grandma Carol looking around at the other present people, waiting to see who walked out of the grave next. And Sam, still patient, still sitting silently, leaned over his knees, his elbows resting on the tops of his thighs, his eyebrows waiting, furrowed in anticipation, politely questioning with his face if he could claim the dead brothers at hand.

"I think they might be my ancestors," said Lillian excitedly. "Are they speaking French?"

"No," said the medium. "They're not speaking French and they're not your ancestors. They're responding negatively to your energy."

Lillian gave a little audible guffaw, looked at Phyllis, and blinked her eyes rapidly.

"Spirits don't care what you want," said the medium. "They come here because they want something from you."

Lillian crossed her arms and legs a little and leaned back into her chair and projected the bodily stance of,

"What a bunch of crock. If I say they're my ancestors, they're my ancestors! What gives you the authority to tell me who these spirits belong to?"

"I think they want something from you," said the medium, looking at Sam. "Actually they're circling around you, kind of yelling at you. One of them just tried to poke his finger in your ear."

"What the fuck," said Sam. "Get them away from me."

"I can't," said the medium. "Maybe it would be best if you lay down so they can properly assess you."

"Like a dog," said Sam.

"You don't have to do it," said the medium.

"I'll lie down," said Sam.

Sam got up from his folding chair and lay down in the middle of the circle. The medium took a bundle of sage and lit it on fire and waved it over Sam's head. Sam closed his eyes and spread his limbs out on the carpet while everyone else watched this performance. Olivia thought he looked dead.

The boys Sam was after were ones he wasn't sure if he had murdered. He'd killed other people at war, but with the others he had always been able to look at their bodies, to assess their corpses and think, here is a thing that was once living that is no longer alive. These boys, though, he could never be sure. It was at long range, with explosives. There was a boom and he had seen body-shaped objects lift off the ground, but whether they were dead—this he did not know. He did not know if they were brothers. He did not know if they were soldiers. They were boys, like him. He kept having dreams about them, as a group, some in which there were hundreds of them and others in which there were just two or three, and his dreams alternated between being a world in which they were alive, recovering, transferring crates of produce on and off a truck bed in a mountain, and a world in which they were all dead. In the dream of the dead, he became one of the boys and saw his body in a hole being shoveled full until it was all black with dirt and he could not see. So there were these two different realities of the boys dead or the boys alive, which he became, periodically, stuck in, and he just wanted one to sit with, which was what the medium was giving him, the fact that they were all dead.

This was what he had come for and he was relieved that it was being delivered to him. Lying down on the floor as sage smoke came into his nose, he could feel his muscles that touched the carpet, which muscles pressed against the warm of the floor, and which parts of his body, like the backs of his knees and the crooks of his ankles, were lifted up off the carpet because the structure of his body's bones would not let them touch.

"Can everyone hum for me please?" said the medium. "*Hmmmmmm.*"

Anna started in with vigor, so Cliff followed, and Olivia and Phyllis went willingly, while Izzy, Carol and especially Lillian were slow to follow but eventually joined in. The buzz of their voices sounded like bees hustling. It went on for a long time like that until the medium stopped and then everyone stopped and Sam got up and went back to his seat.

The sage had smoked up the house and everyone's

voices were sore from humming. There was a sudden feeling of closeness in the ensuing silence, because everyone present had participated, and helped Sam accomplish his thing. What exactly had been done, they weren't sure, but it felt good to have made a sound together for a period of time. This is why, Cliff thought, people like to sing.

The medium had her eyes still closed when she said, "A cat. I usually don't let them in if I see them on Saturdays, but you're not from around here, are you Olivia? And coming back tomorrow would be too hard."

"Thank you," said Olivia. She was glad that the medium hadn't allowed anyone else to try and claim Skillet, a neighborhood kitten that she had adopted earlier in the year and that, less than a week after the adoption, had been run over by a car.

Carol looked surprised. She had decided to take her two granddaughters to the medium because Lillian had wanted to go and Lillian and Carol were something of a duo, and Lillian had pleaded with Carol quietly about it for weeks and Carol liked being pleaded to. So even though Carol didn't particularly care for talking to any spirits and didn't really want to believe, she had gone and dragged her out-of-town visiting granddaughters with her. But now it all seemed kind of silly and things were going poorly because Lillian hadn't seen any of her French relatives and Phyllis was happy as a clam and her youngest granddaughter, Olivia, was now delusionally petting an imaginary cat. Her daughter, the girls' mother, would never forgive her, thought Carol. Good grief! She'd practically handed them over to the cult leader. Izzy looked more skeptical, which reassured her. But who knew what either of her two mysterious granddaughters really had going on inside their heads.

"What a load of bullshit," said Izzy. "How many fourteen-year-olds do you know, who at one point or another, have had a dead cat?" Lillian and Carol nodded in agreement. Everyone else ignored Izzy, most vehemently the medium, who did not even look Izzy's way. Phyllis looked torn.

Anna and Cliff were still huddled together on the far end of the circle, almost directly across from the medium. Cliff held Anna, who periodically touched the sleeping Wilma at both of their feet. Every time Cliff saw Anna touch below her knees it hurt him. Every stroke visibly showed him that he was not enough and that there was a hole and that as good as he was at not being broken he could not do anything for Anna that would fix what had happened and what was wrong. Cliff hoped Anna would not ask him to go back to this trailer with her. If she wanted to come again she would have to come alone.

"This is the last one I'll let in," said the medium. "An old man."

"Don't you think it's Grandpa, Grandma Carol?" said Olivia.

"No I don't," said Carol. "Your Grandpa wouldn't have anything to say."

"I think it's my husband," said Phyllis.

"Don't be ridiculous," said Lillian. "Phyllis, your husband is still alive!"

"It happens," said the medium. "That some souls leave

the bodies they inhabit in stages. Is it possible your husband has already begun to pass on to the next life?"

"Probable," said Phyllis. "I rarely realize he is alive."

"He says he hates you," said the medium.

"Well, I hate him too," said Phyllis, looking strangely satisfied.

"They're all leaving now," said the medium. "Your small hurt girl is getting up and going."

Anna put her head down in Cliff's lap and did not say a word.

"And the foreign brothers and the girl with long blonde hair and the old man. They're all going back into the slit I let them in through," said the medium. "To seal the slit, we'll have to all hold hands."

Joined together in their circle of hand-holding, everyone looked very weary, especially Phyllis, Sam and Anna. On the way out the door the medium spritzed them each with holy water to keep the ghosts from following them outside her home.

It's a strange thing, the medium thought, the way we take care of our living. And even stranger how the living choose to take care of their dead. As she cleaned up her living room and put away the folding chairs she saw Olivia crouched over her dead kitten, it buried in the backyard, put into a hole on a bed of flowers. She saw Phyllis's husband dead in five years, his corpse in a staunch Protestant funeral march, and Carol's childhood friend Alice, syringe in purple arm. She saw Wilma, little and smashed in her tiny coffin, and Sam's foreign brothers howling, lying down legless where they bled to death, and where their bodies stayed until someone found the remains days later and stacked their corpses into a funeral mound like closely pressed strips of dried meat.

And the medium thought of the many ways in which one can come in and out of this life. She thought of the Catholic embalmers ready for the second coming, ready at will to wake up and walk again, stiff lips and an empty head without the brains which have been put in a separate bucket, pulled out of the body through the nose. And then she thought of the Tibetans that cut up their dead into a million pieces and feed the body-bits to the vultures, put their dead right back into the god-system as soon as they can so that the next life will be faster coming, faster found, so that the dead can enter the next body they want to be in before their old body even gets cold in the stomach pit of a big bird. And she thought of those white flocks of families on the banks of the Ganges, their dead painted in gold and red and put on a pile to burn and float downstream. The medium went to Banaras once and saw burning after burning. A black cloud of human flesh smoke had hung over the entire city. People everywhere, either stoic or crying, and everyone in white, everyone with flowers, everyone singing, praying, and the small little boy who could tell she wasn't from there saying, "Come here, *gorah*, this way, let me show you the dead." When the medium thought of her body and what it would look like when she left it, she wished she'd never had it in the same way that someone would regret buying an ill-fitting dress. It seemed to her so unbecoming, to have a body that is only of use temporarily, that after it is done with will be disposed. She thought of the living bodies which had been in her trailer only moments earlier (Phyllis, Carol, Lillian, Izzy, Olivia, Anna, Cliff, and Sam), and she pictured herself cutting open each of their brain containers so that what was truly in their heads became revealed. And she saw herself dipping into each of their brain buckets with a ladle and pulling out from the depths of their bowls their thoughts, which looked like sticky thick woolen thread.

ACKNOWLEDGMENTS

Thanks are owed to the following.

Institutions
A Strange Object
Brown University
Hawthornden Castle
Tent: Creative Writing
The Bread Loaf Writers' Conference
The Helene Wurlitzer Foundation
The MacDowell Colony
The Ruth Asawa San Francisco School of the Arts
The Sewanee Writers' Conference

The Sri Aurobindo Society
Vanderbilt University

People
Adrianne Harun
Alyson Sinclair
Audrey Bullwinkel
Chris Cohen
Clay Bullwinkel
Denise Bullwinkel
Diane Williams
Elana Siegel
Gillian Brassil
Jill Meyers
Joanna Howard
Karina Mudd
Kristina Moore
Laura MacMillan
Laura van den Berg
LB + JG
Lorrie Moore
Lindsey Drager
Maria Anderson
Meg Weeks
Michelle Wildgen
Nancy Reisman
Patty Yumi Cottrell
Raluca Albu
Rebekah Bergman
Sam Lipsyte
Sasha West

Objects

Chris Cohen's 1990 Mazda Miata convertible (generously on loan to me June 2016–August 2016)

Taryn Simon's *A Living Man Declared Dead and Other Chapters I–XVIII*

Lovers

Alex Spoto

ABOUT THE AUTHOR

Rita Bullwinkel's writing has been published in *Tin House*, *BOMB*, *Conjunctions*, *Vice*, *NOON*, and *Guernica*. She is a recipient of grants and fellowships from the Mac-Dowell Colony, Brown University, Vanderbilt University, Hawthornden Castle, and the Helene Wurlitzer Foundation. Both her fiction and her translation have been nominated for Pushcart Prizes. She lives in San Francisco. This is her first book.

ABOUT A STRANGE OBJECT

Founded in 2012, A Strange Object is a women-run, fiction-focused press in Austin, Texas. The press champions debuts, daring writing, and good design across all platforms. Its titles are distributed by Small Press Distribution.